NEW YORK REVIEW BOOKS
CLASSICS

D0911952

TROPIC MOON

GEORGES SIMENON (1903–1989) was born in Liège, Belgium. His father was an insurance salesman, easygoing and unambitious; his mother, an unhappy, angry woman whose coldness and disapproval haunted her son. Simenon went to work as a reporter at the age of fifteen and in 1923 moved to Paris, where under various pseudonyms he became a highly successful and prolific author of pulp fiction while leading a dazzling social life in the company of his first wife and lovers such as the American dancer Josephine Baker. (He is said to have broken up with Baker because their affair was a distraction: he had produced a mere twelve novels during the year.) In the early 1930s, Simenon emerged as a writer under his own name, gaining renown for his detective stories featuring Inspector Maigret. He also began to write his psychological novels, or *romans durs*—books in which he displays his remarkable talent for capturing the look and mood of a place (whether West Africa, the Soviet Union, New York City, or provincial France) together with an acutely sympathetic awareness of the emotional and spiritual pain underlying the routines of daily life. Simenon remained in France throughout the Second World War, at the end of which he was accused of collaboration with the Germans; though quickly cleared of the charges, he moved to America, where he married his second wife and lived for close to a decade, returning to Europe in 1955. Having written nearly two hundred books under his own name and become the best-selling author in the world, whose stories had served as the inspiration for countless movies and TV shows, Simenon retired as a novelist in 1973, devoting himself instead to dictating memoirs that filled thousands of pages: "I consider myself less and less a writer . . . All this is nothing but chatter . . . Since dictating has become a need, so to speak, I will dictate every morning whatever comes into mind . . . I would like to be able to be silent."

NORMAN RUSH is the author of *Whites*, *Mating*, and *Mortals*.

TROPIC MOON

GEORGES SIMENON

Translated from the French by
MARC ROMANO

Introduction by
NORMAN RUSH

NEW YORK REVIEW BOOKS

New York

THIS IS A NEW YORK REVIEW BOOK
PUBLISHED BY THE NEW YORK REVIEW OF BOOKS
1755 Broadway, New York, NY 10019
www.nyrb.com

Simenon, Georges, 1903–
  [Coup de lune. English]
  Tropic moon / by Georges Simenon ; introduction by Norman Rush ;
translated by Marc Romano.
      p. cm. — (New York Review Books classics)
  ISBN 1-59017-111-X (alk. paper)
  I. Romano, Marc. II. Title. III. Series.
  PQ2637.I53C613 2005
  843'.912—dc22

                                    2005006143

ISBN 1-59017-111-X

Printed in the United States of America on acid-free paper.
10 9 8 7 6 5 4 3 2 1

INTRODUCTION

Tropic moon (*Le Coup de lune*) is the first of Georges Simenon's novels to be set outside Europe, and it is also among the first and best of his serious novels, those he called *romans durs* in order to distinguish them from the hundreds of genre fictions he produced, the *romans populaires* that were making him rich and world famous, which included his psychological crime thrillers and the titles in the Inspector Maigret series. It is a remarkable work, in which Simenon's characters deliver a brutal and clueless enactment of interwar French imperialism at its most naked—in Gabon, French West Africa, in the capital Libreville and upcountry. As a revelation of the institutionalized squalor the French Empire amounted to, it stands high, ranking with L. F. Céline's depiction of life in another part of the same empire, Cameroon, in his *Journey to the End of the Night*.

It's a particularity of the iconography in porn magazines that the male partners of the lovingly detailed women on display will often enough be represented essentially as mere functioning lower selves, torsos, their heads cut off by the edges of the layouts. Something similar is seen in the character embodiments in this moral tale: the actors are reduced to their appetites. The face of Adèle, the hyperpromiscuous antiheroine of the novel, is never described. We do learn about her that she wears clinging dresses and disdains underwear. She is in her thirties. Her breasts droop, slightly. Similarly, the African locale is rendered rather generically. We have the Hotel, the Prefecture, the Docks, the Police Station, all evoked without recourse to the kind of detail that might distract from the vertiginous drama of personal destruction we have come to witness. Simenon's heightened minimalism serves his purposes well, forwarding the staccato unfolding of the central plot. Maddening heat, isolation, boredom, illness, alcohol—the traditional scourges of white expatriates in tropical Africa—play their expected parts in sustaining the lethal malaise that hangs over Libreville.

Joseph Timar, a young man from the provinces (La Rochelle), arrives in Libreville in the early 1930s intending to take up a posting at a timber camp in the jungle. His well-placed family in France has arranged this opportunity for him. He is an innocent. Obstacles arise that prevent him from going directly upriver and he falls into a sexual relationship, not an affair exactly, with the wife of the owner of the hotel he is lodging in. This is Adèle, and she has been active with a great many of the French gentlemen around town. Billiards, Pernod, card games, out-of-date newspapers, and intermittent sex with Adèle occupy Timar's time. When the mood seizes them, male members of the French community organize orgies in the bush with native women, abandoning them there without transportation at the end of the one excursion Timar goes along on. At this stage, the story has only begun. To come are rape, corrupt legal proceedings, other varieties of chicanery, more death, more spectacles of injustice.

We can't help but read this novel today against our knowledge that in 1932 European civilization is poised, one more time, to give birth to monstrous fratricide, genocide, apocalyptic warfare, cultural destruction, the breaking of nations. In *Tropic Moon* the dehumanizing heedlessness, rapacity, and cruelty shown by the agents of the French *mission civilatrice* toward the black populations under their control will, we know, be replicated, played out differently very soon elsewhere, by different Europeans, different actors, with different victims. And beyond the looming specter of fascism—a subject, by the way, not on the minds of any of the characters in this book—is something else we know is coming. And that something else is the bleak outcome for black Africa of the inevitable arrival of independence, a process itself hastened by the autodestruction of European power. The reader is barred from the easy comfort of feeling that the poverty and cruelty of colonial life described in Simenon's novel will be, will have been, undone by decolonization. Conditions in West Africa today are dauntingly, if variably, grim. But how could it be otherwise? The scene presented by Simenon—the stripping of natural resources by French commercial interests, the instruction in unfairness provided by the colonial system of justice, the reduction of the African population to servile status—is portentous. There are portents in *Tropic Moon*. Its original readers may not have seen them, but we do.

In the matter of justice, Simenon's novels—the *romans durs* and the psychological crime studies—dispense with it. It is not to be had, generally speaking. So *Tropic Moon* can be taken as one more specimen from a dense array of similarly Hobbesian Simenon stories set anywhere, including the United States, Europe, ships at sea, in which crimes (typically crimes of passion or impulse) are committed, *l'homme nu* (Simenon's term for the potentially murderous universal everyman he saw everywhere and in every station of life) does his thing, people get hurt, and somebody's suicide may wrap things up. If you want to see justice done, you must go to the seventy-six Maigret *policiers*. Maigret embodies justice, the bringing of order. Simenon referred to him as *le redresseur des destins*. Maigret is reliable. Simenon kept the two streams of narrative running fiercely side by side, his whole life. It makes an interesting balance. Graham Greene, another great writer as engaged as Simenon with questions of crime and punishment, made a similar distinction between his commercial products, which he called entertainments, and his serious novels. Greene, however, employed his serious novels as vehicles for explorations of justice—justifications of the ways of God to man. There is no theodicy in Simenon. Nothing close.

It can be instructive to compare what a novel stands for or represents—its direct or implicit advocacies or critiques—and what it accomplishes as a strictly aesthetic device. *Tropic Moon* is notable on both counts. What it achieves aesthetically is a true evocation of a social hell and a persuasive portrayal of what it does to thinking, perception, identity to be a member of the oppressor class in such an environment, and, to a lesser degree, of what the toll is on the oppressed. This evocation is conveyed in Simenon's trademark style—swift, colloquial, seamless. (Simenon deliberately restricted his literary vocabulary to two thousand words, in the interest of accessibility.)

What *Tropic Moon* represents politically is a thunderous and absolute blast against empire as it was then. The novel arose out of travel reports Simenon wrote for the magazine *Voilà* in 1932, a series published under the title *L'Afrique vous parle: elle vous dit merde.* Simenon's summary conclusion, according to his biographer Patrick Marnham, was essentially that colonialism was not practical. Marnham writes,

> In years to come he was to recount many times how he had always seen through colonialism, and even before his journey through Africa had been a resolute opponent of it. In fact what he wrote . . . (on the subject) was both more complicated and more original . . . His conclusion was that colonialism was a fraud and that it would have been better to leave the people of Africa in peace than to make any attempt to introduce education or medical care or democratic government . . . Simenon's chief objection to colonialism at the time, was for the effect it had on the white colonials.

The complications in Simenon's anticolonialism don't end there. What exactly did he think he was doing when he ran backstage after a birthday performance given for him by a Martiniquaise dance troupe and had his way with two of the dancers, to general merriment? It's hard not to think of Simenon as a rich, entitled white erotomane first and an anticolonialist second. In any case, his magazine series and *Tropic Moon* incited resentment in official circles, and when he sought to revisit the French colonies in 1936, he was denied a visa.

An aspect of empire that Simenon captures well is the ethical blankness, the cloud of unknowing, it seems to engender in the psyches of the imperializers, at all levels. The characters in *Tropic Moon* may experience odd moments of vague disquiet that interrupt the peculiar emotional equilibrium that reigns while dark deeds are routinely transpiring, but deep recognition of what is truly happening is rare, and when it occurs, costly. The conditions floridly depicted by Simenon, specific though they may be to a time and a place in the past, are not irrelevant for Americans to contemplate in the new millennium. Here, writing in 1921 in his book *The New World*, is Isaiah Bowman, Director of the American Geographic Society and a high-level adviser to a string of American presidents on matters of global policy:

> United States expansion has in recent years evoked a certain hostility...Here we have a problem of the first rank. For the people of the United States are as unknown to themselves as they are to the rest of the world. They do not know how they will take interference in their policy of expansion...

Today, something very much resembling empire is back. It remains to be seen how our own fictions will serve us now and how they will be read in the future.

—NORMAN RUSH

TROPIC MOON

I

WAS THERE really any reason for him to be so anxious? No. Nothing out of the ordinary had happened. Nothing threatened him. It was ridiculous to feel this way. He knew it—knew it so well that even now, in the middle of the party, he was struggling to regain his self-control.

Anyway, properly speaking, it wasn't anxiety. He couldn't have pointed to the precise moment when he'd been gripped by this dread, this feeling of unease born of some imperceptible disequilibrium.

Not when he'd left Europe, in any case. On the contrary, Joseph Timar had set out in excellent spirits, flush with enthusiasm.

Was it when he'd gone ashore in Libreville, at his first contact with Gabon? The ship had anchored at the mouth of the harbor, so far offshore that all there was to see of the land was a white streak—the sand—with a streak of dark vegetation above it. Great gray swells lifted the launch and drove it crashing against the ship's lifeboat. Timar was alone at the bottom of the ship's ladder, the water beneath his feet, staring at the dinghy, which rose toward him only to be washed away again a second later.

A naked arm, a black arm, had seized him. Then he'd set off with the black, bounding over the wave crests. Some fifteen minutes later—perhaps more—they reached a jetty of jumbled concrete blocks. The ship was already sounding its whistle.

There wasn't even a black waiting there. No one. Just Timar in the middle of all his baggage.

That wasn't when he'd started to worry, though. He'd flagged down a passing truck that brought him to the Central, Libreville's only hotel.

What a sight! This was the real Africa! In the café with the African masks on the wall, Timar cranked up the old gramophone. He felt like a real colonial.

As for the great event, that had been more funny than dramatic. Talk about colonial! But Timar had been taken with everything that was colonial.

Thanks to an uncle, he'd landed a job with SACOVA. In France the head of the company had told him that he'd be living in the middle of the jungle, somewhere not far from Libreville, logging timber and selling cheap goods to the natives.

No sooner had Timar arrived than he hurried off to the run-down factory building with SACOVA on it. With his right hand extended, he approached someone who was either depressed or disgusted, and who looked at Timar's hand without taking it.

"You're the director? Pleased to meet you—I'm your new employee."

"Employed by what? Who employed you? For what? What are you doing here? I don't need anybody."

Timar hadn't flinched. It was the director who was astonished. Behind his glasses his round eyes grew enormous, and he became almost polite. There was something confidential in his manner of speaking.

The same old story once again! The head office in France meddling in the colony's business! As to the post Timar had been promised? That was all the way upriver, ten days' journey by flatboat. But for one thing, the flatboat's hull was staved in and wouldn't be ready for at least a month. For another, the post was occupied by a crazy old man who'd promised to shoot the first replacement sent his way.

"Work it out for yourself. It's none of my business."

There'd been four days of it, all four days that Joseph Timar had been in Africa. He knew Libreville better than La Rochelle, where he'd been born: a long esplanade covered in red dust and bordered by palms; the open-air native market; small factory buildings every hundred yards; farther back in the vegetation, a few large villas.

He'd seen the flatboat with the broken hull. Nobody was working on it. Nobody'd been told what to do. Timar, the newcomer and something of a fifth wheel, didn't dare issue any orders himself.

He was twenty-three years old with the manners of a well-brought-up young man. Even the boys who waited tables laughed.

No reason to be anxious? Yes, there was, and he knew what it was. And if he kept going over all these reasons that didn't apply, it was only to put off the moment when he'd get to the one that did.

The reason was there, surrounding him, in the hotel. It was the hotel itself. It was ...

He'd been very taken by the sight of the hotel, a yellow edifice set some fifty yards back from the esplanade and its palm trees and surrounded by a dense growth of curious-looking plants.

The main room was both a café and a restaurant. It had bright pastel walls that reminded him of Provence and a bar of polished mahogany. That and the high stools and the copper countertop added a touch of luxury.

All the bachelors in Libreville took their meals there. Each one had his own table and napkin ring.

Upstairs, the rooms were always available. Vacant, bare rooms, also in pastel, with beds draped in mosquito netting, and, here and there, an old pitcher, a cracked basin, an empty steamer trunk.

Everywhere, upstairs and down, the drawn venetian blinds sliced up the sun. The whole house was filled with bands of shadow and light.

Timar's luggage was the luggage of a young man from a good family. It looked strange on the floor of the room. He wasn't used to washing in a small basin. Above all, he wasn't used to finding a bush to take care of his other needs.

He wasn't used to the teeming creatures: the unfamiliar flies, the flying scorpions, the hairy spiders.

And that first attack of gnawing unease pursued him tenaciously, like a cloud of insects. At night, with his candle out, he could see the pale mosquito netting around him like a cage in the dark. Above, he sensed an immense void broken by rustlings, half-audible noises, fragile creatures—was it a scorpion, a mosquito, a spider?—that sometimes settled on the transparent gauze.

And in the middle of that soft cage, he tried to keep track of the sounds, the quiverings in the air, to take note of the sudden silences.

Abruptly he lifted himself up on his elbows. It was morning. The rays of sunlight were already there. The door had just opened. Smiling and sedate, the woman who ran the hotel was looking at him.

Timar was naked. He realized it only then. His sweaty shoulders and chest emerged from the rumpled sheets. Why was he naked? He struggled to remember.

He'd been very hot, sweating heavily. He'd searched in vain for matches. Creatures seemed to be crawling on his skin.

That must have been it—no doubt sometime in the middle of the night—the moment when he'd taken off his pajamas. Now she could see his white skin, his exposed rib cage. She seemed extraordinarily self-possessed as she shut the door behind her. "Sleep well?" she asked.

Timar's pants lay on the floor. She lifted them, shook out the dust, and put them on a chair.

Timar was afraid to get up. His bed stank of sweat. There was dirty water in the basin; the comb was missing several teeth.

Still, he didn't want her to leave—this woman in a black nightgown who was smiling at him very gently and a little ironically, too.

"I came to ask you what you like to drink in the morning. Coffee? Tea? Cocoa? Did your mother used to wake you up back in Europe?"

She'd pulled back the mosquito netting and was making fun of him. She was teasing him, smiling so broadly that he could see her teeth. Maybe she really did want to take a bite out of him.

Because he was different from the colonials, lying there in bed with his look of well-groomed adolescence.

She wasn't being forward. She wasn't being maternal, either. And yet there was something of both there—and, more than anything, a mute sensuality filling the ample flesh of this woman of thirty-some years.

Was she naked under the black silk dress? In spite of his embarrassment, Timar asked himself the question.

At the same time he felt a stab of desire that was reinforced by things that had nothing to do with it, like the bands of light and shadow, the animal clamminess of the sheets, even the restless night he'd endured, with its unknown terrors, its gropings in the dark.

"Look! You've been bitten."

Sitting on the edge of the bed, she placed a finger on his naked breast, touching a little red smudge. She looked Timar in the eyes.

That was what happened. The rest was too quick and too clumsy, marked by awkwardness and mess. She had seemed as surprised as he was, and he'd been completely astonished. Arranging her hair in front of the mirror, she said, "Thomas will bring you your coffee."

Thomas was the boy. For Timar, he was just a black. He was still too new to Africa to tell one black from another.

An hour later, when he went downstairs, she was managing the hotel from behind the bar, crocheting something out of vulgar rose-colored silk. Every trace of their violent, frenzied intimacy had disappeared. She was calm and serene. As always, she was smiling.

"When would you like to have lunch?"

He didn't even know her name! He didn't know what to do with himself. He could barely remember it, above all the feeling of soft skin, of flesh that was not too firm but that he'd savored. A little black woman brought fish to her, and without a word she picked out the best ones. She threw a few coins in the basket.

Her husband's head emerged from the cellar, followed by his powerful body. And yet he seemed tired. He was a giant, but his gestures were feeble, his mouth was twisted with disgust, his eyes were angry.

"You're still here?"

And like an idiot Timar blushed.

This had been going on for three days now. Only she no longer came to his room in the morning. From his bed, he could hear her coming and going in the big room, issuing orders to Thomas, buying provisions from the blacks at the door.

From dawn until dusk she wore the same silk dress. He knew she was naked underneath. It disturbed him so much that he often had to look away.

There was nothing for him to go out and do. He stayed there all day long, almost, drinking whatever there was to drink, reading three-week-old newspapers, playing billiards by himself.

She crocheted and served the people who stopped in for a moment at the bar. Her husband busied himself with the beer and the bottles and with straightening up the tables, sometimes sending Timar to sit in another corner. He looked at him like something that was in the way.

There was a feeling of exasperation and irritability, a sense of darkness in spite of the sun, and the feeling was most intense when it was hottest, when just lifting an arm made you break out in a sweat.

At noon and in the evening, the regulars came to eat dinner and play billiards. Timar didn't know them. They looked at him curiously, without showing goodwill or dislike. He was afraid to say a single word to them.

———

At last it was time for the party, a roaring party. In less than an hour, everyone was drunk—even Timar, who sat sipping his champagne all alone.

A dancer called Manuelo provided the entertainment. He must have arrived at the hotel while Timar was out or asleep. Timar ran into him around eleven in the morning—smiling, friendly, seemingly right at home, Manuelo pasted up posters in the bar proclaiming himself to be the greatest Spanish dancer in the world.

He was a small man, lithe and charming. He already got along very well with the woman, not the way men get along with women but the way women do with one another.

By noon, the tables had been rearranged to make room for Manuelo's dances. The room was garlanded with colored paper; the gramophone had been tested.

Up in his room the Spaniard had been practicing his act for hours, stomping loudly on the shaking floor.

Perhaps Timar was annoyed because the usual rhythm of his day had been upset. In spite of the sun, he went out. Under his sun helmet he could feel his head heating up. The black women looked at him and laughed.

The regulars had eaten earlier than usual because of the party. Then outsiders had started to arrive, white men Timar had never seen before, white men and white women—the women in evening gowns—along with two Englishmen in dinner jackets.

Bottles of champagne invaded the tables. Outside in the dark, behind the doors and windows, hundreds of silent blacks suddenly appeared.

Manuelo danced, a dance so feminine that it made him appear all the more epicene. The woman was behind the counter of the bar. Timar knew her name now—Adèle. Everyone called her that and most of them used the familiar "tu." He was probably the only one who addressed her as "madame." Wearing her black silk dress, as always, and naked under it, she'd come up to him.

"Champagne? Will Pieper be good enough for you? I only have

a few bottles of Mumm's left and the Englishmen won't have anything else."

That had made him happy; he'd even been touched. So why did he look so down only a few minutes later? Manuelo had danced a few numbers. Adèle's husband—he was also "tu," or Eugène, to everyone—went and sat down by the gramophone in a corner. He looked surlier than ever. From there he could see and hear everything, calling out to the boys, "Don't you see, idiot, they want drinks over there?"

Then, with unaccustomed care, he lifted the needle on the record. Timar had also been straining to hear, picking up bits and pieces of conversation, trying to make sense of them. But it was nearly impossible. The people at the next table were talking to a large young man, hardly a distinguished figure, who looked like a college student and was on his tenth whiskey. They kept calling him "Mr. Prosecutor." Some loggers were saying: "As long as you make sure not to leave any evidence, you're in the clear. And it's easy—just spread a wet handkerchief on his back. After that, you can let him have it. The whip doesn't leave a trace."

They meant the back of a black man, of course!

———

Had Timar already drained an entire bottle? He'd been given another and his glass was full again. He could see partway into the kitchen. Just then Adèle hit Thomas in the face with her fist. What? The black didn't flinch; he took the blow without moving, his eyes staring straight ahead.

They played the same tunes ten times over. A few couples danced. Most people had taken their jackets off.

Outside the silent throng of blacks went on watching the whites at play.

Adèle's husband sat by the gramophone. His features were drawn. His stare was so hard that his face looked like a tragic mask.

What was going on? Nothing, it seemed. It had been a mistake for Timar to drink so much. Suddenly all his little worries rose to the surface, all the bad impressions he'd formed about the last few days.

He wanted to say something to Adèle, no matter what, if only to make contact. He glanced around. He followed her with his eyes. He couldn't get her to look at him. Then she came by on her way to another table. She walked right past him, and he pricked up his courage, snagging her dress in his fingers.

A moment of stopped time. A look. A single sentence: "What are you waiting there for when you should be asking your boss's wife for a dance?"

He followed the inclination of her chin to a fat housewife in a pink dress sitting beside the SACOVA manager. Why had Adèle said that? And with such an edge? Was she jealous? He was afraid to hope for so much. In any case, he hadn't even looked at another woman.

She was talking to customers and smiling her usual smile. She returned to her cash register. She walked toward the back of the café, where the door opened out onto the courtyard. No one noticed except Timar, who unconsciously drained another glass.

"I'm such a fool! To think I was the only one!"

He would have given a lot, just then, to hold her in his arms, hot and sweaty, with her almost liquid flesh, her waist that, for an instant, had seemed so flexible it beggared belief.

How many minutes went by? Five? Ten? Adèle's husband, with his tragic look, cranked up the gramophone one more time. Timar noticed a bottle of mineral water beside him.

Adèle didn't come back. Eugène—perhaps aware of her absence —was looking around for someone.

Timar rose, then paused. He was astonished to feel so light-headed. Crossing the room lengthwise, he reached the little door, the courtyard, then another door leading outside. Someone ran into him with a crash. It was Adèle.

He stammered, "At last—"

"Get out of the way, you idiot!"

Total darkness; a few strains of music: the black dress disappeared. He was left standing there, lost, frustrated, and miserable.

The clock read three. Manuelo had long since finished dancing and was counting his money now. Dressed as a man again, he was drinking crème de menthe at one of the tables and talking about his successes in Casablanca, Dakar, and the Belgian Congo.

At the bar Adèle was refilling glasses, her forehead furrowed in concentration.

The prosecutor was sitting at the bar between the two Englishmen. He was drunk and sarcastic.

A lot of people had left. At two of the tables, loggers were drinking beer and eating sandwiches.

"Enough of that music!" one of them shouted. "Turn it off, Eugène, and come have a drink."

Adèle's husband stood up, his lips strangely twisted. He looked at the mess in the café—the party streamers strewn on the floor, the empty glasses, the stained tablecloths—and his eyes shone feverishly. As he walked toward the door, he seemed dizzy. He kept going, muttering, "I'll be right back."

Adèle was counting banknotes. She bundled them up and secured them with rubber bands.

Exhausted, drained, and distraught, Timar finished his bottle without thinking. Later no one could say for sure how long Adèle's husband had been gone.

When he did come back, he seemed bigger, bulkier. But he was so feeble that it was funny.

He stood in the doorway and called out, "Adèle!"

His wife looked at him, and kept counting money.

"Is the doctor gone? Call him back, quickly!"

A long silence. His voice again. "Where's Thomas? I don't see him."

Timar looked around, like the others. There were only the two young boys who'd been hired for the party.

"You don't look so great," ventured one of the loggers.

Adèle's husband gave him a look that could kill.

"Shut up!" he said slowly. "Got it? Bring the doctor, if he's not too drunk. I'm screwed anyway. Snail fever."

Timar didn't understand, but the customers plainly did. Hurriedly they rose to their feet.

"Eugène, you—"

Eugène's voice was weary.

"All of you, get out. It's time to close the place."

And he disappeared down the hall. A door slammed. There was a noise like someone kicking over a chair.

Looking pale, Adèle lifted her head. She was listening to a faint sound coming nearer and beginning to grow clear. A group of four or five blacks showed up at the door.

Timar didn't understand what they were saying. It was just a few words, squeezed out syllable by syllable from their mouths.

But he heard the one-eyed logger translating: "They just found Thomas's body. He's been shot and killed—two hundred yards from here."

Upstairs there was the sound of someone pounding on the floor with a cane. Eugène was impatient. Finally, he climbed out of bed and opened his door to shout, "Adèle! Are you just going to let me die up here, for God's sake?"

2

THE MOSQUITO net had fallen down, and Timar woke up with it knotted around him. The room was full of sunlight. It was always sunny here, but the sunlight was joyless.

Sitting on his bed, he listened to the household noises. During the night, half asleep, he'd heard comings and goings, whisperings, the sound of water splashing into a china pitcher.

When the doctor appeared, Adèle had told Timar to go upstairs and shooed away the others.

"If you need me..." he'd stammered foolishly.

"Okay! I hear you! Now go to bed!"

Was Adèle's husband dead, as he'd said he was sure to be? Someone was sweeping the café in any case. Opening his door a crack, Timar heard Adèle say, "There isn't any Gruyère left? And there's none at the store? So open up a can of green beans! Wait! For dessert, bananas and apricot—the right-hand row. Do you understand, you fool?"

She hadn't raised her voice. She wasn't in a bad mood. She always spoke to the blacks like that.

A few minutes later, unshaven, Timar went downstairs. He found Adèle at the cash register, sorting receipts. Around her everything was clean and in its usual order. Adèle was neatly dressed. Her black dress wasn't wrinkled. Her hair was combed.

"What time is it?" he asked, taken aback.

"Just past nine."

And her husband's attack had started at four in the morning! The café had been a mess then. Adèle hadn't slept, and yet here she was asking about cheese and fruit, with the menu for lunch all prepared!

But she was paler than she normally was, and there were narrow rings under her eyes that changed her appearance. Under her dress, though, you could still make out her breasts. Timar blushed without knowing why.

"Is your husband feeling better?"

She looked at him in surprise, and seemed to recall that he'd only been in the colony for four days.

"He won't last out the day."

"Where is he?"

She glanced at the ceiling. He was afraid to ask if the sick man was up there all alone, but she guessed his thoughts.

"He's starting to rave. He's no longer aware of anything. By the way, there's a note for you."

She looked around on the counter and handed it to him: a small official note requesting the said Joseph Timar to present himself at the police station at his earliest convenience.

A black woman came in carrying a basket of eggs. Adèle shook her head no.

"You'd better go now, before it gets too hot."

"What do you think they—"

"You'll find out soon enough."

She wasn't worried. Like her, the café seemed no different from any other morning.

"Turn right after the pier; it's just before you get to United Shipping. Wait—your sun helmet!"

Maybe he was imagining things. Yet he could have sworn that the blacks were acting strangely that morning. At the market there was the usual chatter and rainbow array of loincloths. But suddenly someone in the crowd would fix him with a stare. Four or five of the natives would fall silent and turn to look.

Timar quickened his pace. He was beginning to sweat. He made a wrong turn and found himself in front of the governor's house. He retraced his steps until at last, at the end of a badly marked street, he saw a shack with a sign in front of it: POLICE STATION.

It was childishly written in white paint, and the "s" in "station" was reversed. Barefoot blacks in police uniforms were sitting on the steps of the veranda. A typewriter was clacking in the shady interior.

"The chief of police, please."

"Your summons..."

Out on the veranda, Timar looked for the note while he stood waiting. Then he was called into an office where the venetian blinds were closed.

"Have a seat. You're Joseph Timar?"

In the dimness, he finally made out a red-faced man with bulging eyes.

"When did you come to Libreville? Have a seat!"

"I came on the last boat, Wednesday."

"You aren't, by chance, related to Counselor General Timar?"

"He's my uncle."

All of a sudden, the police chief rose. He pushed back his chair, reached out a soft hand, and, in an entirely different tone, repeated, "Have a seat. He still lives in Cognac? I was an inspector there for five years."

Timar was relieved. In this dark and cluttered room, his initial impulse had been to feel outrage or dismay. There were some five hundred whites in Libreville—people who'd committed themselves to hard, sometimes dangerous lives, all for what in France was described, with particular emphasis, as "the exploitation of the colonies."

But as for him, no sooner was he off the boat than he'd been summoned by the chief of police and treated like a tramp!

"Your uncle's a good man. He could be a senator anytime he wants. But what did you come here for?"

It was the police chief's turn to be astonished, so astonished that Timar was worried.

"I signed a contract with SACOVA."

"The director's leaving?"

"Oh no. At least in theory, I'm meant to have the river posting, but—"

Now, instead of astonishment, it was stupefaction.

"Does your uncle know?"

"He was the one who got me the posting. One of his friends is the administrator of—"

Timar was still in his chair. The police chief walked around him and examined him with interest. When he crossed through a ray of sunlight, you could see that his upper lip was cleft. His face and profile were more rugged than they'd seemed at first.

"What a strange idea! Well, we'll talk about it again later. Did you know the Renauds before you arrived?"

"The Renauds?"

"The owners of the Central . . . speaking of which, has he died yet?"

"It seems he won't last out the afternoon."

"Good heavens! And . . ."

Suddenly Timar realized what was bothering him about the police chief's manner, in spite of his cordiality. As he paced back and forth in the office, he kept looking at Timar the same way Adèle did.

Surprised, intrigued, even a little tenderly.

"Would you care for a whiskey?"

Without waiting for an answer, he ordered it from one of the boys out on the veranda.

"And, of course, you have no more idea what happened last night than any of the others."

Timar blushed, and the police chief noticed. Timar blushed even more deeply. His interlocutor took the bottle of liquor from the black and filled two glasses, panting the whole time, as if overwhelmed by the heat.

"You're not unaware that someone killed a black no more than two hundred yards from the hotel. I've informed the governor. It's a nasty business, a very nasty business."

Someone was still tapping away in the room next door. The door was open, and Timar noted that the typist was black.

"Cheers. You can't understand—but over the next few days you'll begin to. I'll have to have you in for questioning, like the others. Everyone will tell me the same thing, which is that they know nothing about it. A cigarette? No? You'll have to come over for lunch soon, and I'll introduce you to my wife. She's from Calvados, but she knew your uncle, too, in Cognac."

Timar relaxed. Now he liked the dimness that he'd found so disturbing at first. The whiskey made him feel better yet. And the police chief was no longer staring: he'd gotten a good enough look. Timar ventured a question.

"The Renauds you mentioned before—who are they?"

"Fifteen years ago, Eugène Renaud was sent into administrative exile from France. For white slavery, mainly, but probably there were a few other reasons, too. There are others like him in Libreville."

"And his wife?"

"Well, she's his wife! What else can I say? She was already with him back then. For the most part they worked around the Terns. Bottoms up!"

Timar drained his glass three times, maybe four. The police chief drank just as much. Soon he was chatty. If a phone call from the prosecutor about an urgent matter hadn't come, the conversation would have gone on a lot longer.

Timar left when the sun was at its height. It was so oppressive that after a hundred yards he felt scared. The nape of his neck was burning. The whiskey wasn't sitting too well with him, and he kept thinking about Eugène Renaud's snail fever and the other stories he'd just heard.

Most of all he was thinking about Adèle: when he was just seven years old she was already helping Renaud spirit girls off to South America. She'd followed Renaud to Gabon when there'd been nothing along the coast but wooden shacks. They'd gone into the jungle—the only whites for days and days in any direction by skiff. They'd started logging and sending the timber downriver.

Timar turned it all into naïve images—illustrations out of Jules Verne mixed up with bits and pieces of reality. He followed the long red dirt path by the shore; he could see the palm trees outlined against the sky and the lead gray of the sea. There were no waves and hardly a ripple—just one, like the curve of a lip, extending the length of the beach. Colorful loincloths and half-naked men surrounded the fishermen's skiffs that had just come in.

The river was over there, at the lower end of the bay, less than half a mile away. Back in the heroic times of Eugène and Adèle, there'd been no merchants' houses or government buildings here, their red roofs mixed in among the greenery.

She must have worn boots and an ammunition belt. Surely not a black silk dress over her naked body.

He tried to walk in the shade, but it was just as hot there as in the sun. The air was scorching; even his clothes were hot to the touch. Back then, they hadn't had brick walls—or ice to cool a drink.

After eight years, and in defiance of the administrative order, Eugène and Adèle had returned to France with six hundred thousand francs. In a few months, they'd spent them. "Blown it all," the police chief said.

On what? What sort of life had they led? Where might Timar, barely pubescent, have run into them?

They'd gone back to Africa—back into the jungle. Eugène had had two attacks of snail fever. Adèle nursed him through them.

They'd bought the Central only three years ago.

Timar had held her in his arms one morning, on the edge of a sweaty bed.

He didn't dare take off his sun helmet to wipe his forehead. It was noon and he was the only one walking along that burning path. There was absolutely no one else.

The police chief had told him other stories about other people, not at all indignantly, though he grumbled that they went too far.

Like the plantation owner last month. Thinking that his cook had tried to poison him, he'd hung him by his feet over a washtub. From time to time he would lower the cook's head into the water. Then for more than fifteen minutes he'd forgotten to pull him out. The cook had died.

The trial was still going on. The League of Nations had stepped in. And now another native had been killed.

"There's nothing we can do for them," the police chief had declared.

"For who?"

"The killers."

"And the other times?"

"It's usually possible to arrange something."

When Adèle left the house on the night of the party, what had she gone out to do? And why, a few hours earlier, had she struck Thomas in the face?

Timar hadn't said anything about it. He wasn't going to. But hadn't there been other people who'd seen her coming in from outside?

But once again he'd lost his way; he'd have to retrace his steps. Finally he got back to the hotel, where for once the clinking sound of cutlery wasn't accompanied by the usual noontime murmurs of conversation. They all looked up at him. Noticing that Adèle wasn't there, he went and sat down at his table.

The boy was a new one, very young. Someone tugged Timar's sleeve. Turning around, he saw it was one of the loggers, the biggest one, who had the head and profile of a butcher.

"It's all over."

"What?"

A nod toward the ceiling.

"He kicked it. By the way, what did he say to you?"

Everything was happening too fast, especially in this stupefying noon heat. Timar couldn't get his thoughts straight. He knew he looked ridiculous asking, "Who?"

"The chief of police! He summoned you first because he figured it'd be easier to grill a newcomer. This afternoon or tomorrow, it's going to be our turn."

No one stopped eating, but all eyes were fixed on Timar. He didn't know what to say. He was upset by the thought of the dead man up there—Adèle must be watching over him—and by the stories the police chief had told him.

"Did you get the feeling that he knows anything?"

"I couldn't say. I swore I'd seen nothing."

"That's good."

Obviously he'd just earned some points. Now they looked friendlier. But did they know he knew something? Did they know, too?

Timar blushed and ate some sausage. He was surprised to hear himself ask, "Did he suffer much?"

Then he realized he shouldn't have asked that question; the suffering must have been terrible.

"The worst thing about it is that it happened right after that hanging business," the one-eyed logger said.

So they were thinking about that, too! Everybody was! Everyone, in other words, was involved, and they were curious and suspicious about Timar because he wasn't.

Footsteps sounded in the room overhead. A door opened and closed. Someone was coming down the stairs.

It was Adèle Renaud. The café was absolutely silent as she walked to the counter and picked up the phone receiver.

She was unchanged, her breasts showing as clearly as ever beneath the silk of her dress. It was childish for him to notice that, but it was what bothered Timar most—as if grief meant wearing a bra.

"Hello? Yes, two-five. Hello? Is Oscar there? Yes, it's me. As soon as he comes in, tell him it's over; he should bring everything he needs. The doctor doesn't want us to keep the body any later than noon tomorrow. No! Thanks, that'll do very well."

After she hung up she stayed where she was for a long time, elbows on the bar, chin on her fists, staring straight ahead. Then, barely turning her head, she spoke to the boy: "Well, why haven't you cleared the table in back yet?"

She opened a drawer and shut it again. She was about to get up and leave, but then she changed her mind. She went back to her earlier pose, her chin on her clenched hands. A voice from the loggers' table asked, "Will he be buried tomorrow?"

"Yes. The doctor says it wouldn't be wise to wait longer."

"If you need help . . ."

"Thanks—everything's taken care of. They're coming with the coffin soon."

She was looking at Timar. He could feel it. He didn't dare raise his eyes.

"Did you see the police chief, Mr. Timar? Was he very unfriendly?"

"No . . . I—he knows my uncle, who's a counselor general, and he—"

He fell silent. Once again he felt himself surrounded by their mocking curiosity, now tinged with a bit of respect, and it unnerved him. And just then he saw it: the soft smile quickly crossing Adèle's sinuous lips.

"I had to move you to another room. I don't have any other to keep the body in tonight."

She turned to the line of bottles behind her, selected a calvados, and poured herself a glass. She drank it with a wince of disgust. Then in a neutral voice she asked, "What did they do with the black?"

"Took him to the hospital. They're performing the autopsy this afternoon. It seems that the bullet came out between the shoulder blades. It hasn't been found yet."

The logger's words were pronounced with distinct intent. He shrugged and swallowed an apricot half that looked like the yolk of an egg, then went on: "There's a black policeman on the scene to prevent anyone from coming for the bullet if it's found. *If* it's found. Anyone for a billiards game?"

Wiping his mouth with a napkin, he stood. Confronted by the general silence, he muttered, "Maybe not today. Give me a calvados, Adèle."

And he leaned his elbows on the counter across from her while the others finished their meal. Timar's cheeks flushed. He ate mechanically. A fly was buzzing around him; each time it passed by he felt a spasm of anger.

The atmosphere was heavy. Not a breath of air outside. You couldn't even hear the thin rippling of the sea nearby.

Nothing but the occasional clatter of plates at the opening to the kitchen. The first to go was the assistant director of the bank, a large young man whose manners bore some resemblance to Timar's and who ate his meals at the hotel. He put on his sun helmet, lit a cigarette, and left.

The others soon followed, some stopping at the bar for a drink on their way out. By the time the clock struck two, only Timar and Adèle would be left in the café.

Timar wondered if he'd stay until then. The four whiskies he'd drunk that morning had made him sluggish. His head was empty and aching, but he didn't feel up to sleeping in a new room while the body was moved into his.

Someone asked, drink in hand, "Is there going to be a viewing before they close the coffin?"

"I don't think so. It'll be all over by five."

"Poor old fellow!"

The person speaking was the same age as Adèle's husband. Some of the younger men had already had their second attack of fever. The police chief had told Timar that quite a few of them had made fortunes and gone back to France to spend them in less than a year. There was a time when the one-eyed logger with the gold tooth had been in Bordeaux on the night of a big gala at the opera; he'd hired all the taxis in town just to watch the people in their fancy dress walk home in a driving rain. Now, after an attack of fever, he scraped by making light deliveries in a little old truck and doing odd jobs for the department of public works.

A factory bell sounded 1:30. Only three or four people were left in the café. Still at his table, Timar was staring at the floor.

The last drinker drained his glass and took his sun helmet from the hat rack. Timar's heart began to beat faster, and he wondered anxiously what they were going to say to each other.

The footsteps trailed off in the distance. With enormous effort, he raised his head. He'd decided to have a drink himself—resigned to oblivion for the rest of the day.

Just then Adèle sighed like someone with an unwelcome task ahead. He heard her close the drawer of the cash register. Without saying anything to him or looking at him, she went out. For another instant he saw her through the opening to the kitchen: she was issuing orders in a low voice. At last she headed upstairs. Her footsteps echoed over Timar's head.

3

DINNER was more or less the same as lunch, except that the body upstairs was no longer lying in bed but in a coffin supported by two chairs.

The regulars exchanged knowing glances, as if to remind one another of a pact they'd made. When the meal was over, the logger with the butcher's face came up to the counter.

"Say, Adèle, don't you think it would be better to close up?"

"That's what I'm planning to do."

"And … I guess … someone will be watching over the body? If you want, obviously, you can rely on us."

It was comical, the contrast between his brutal appearance and his childish expression, like a schoolboy asking permission for something.

"Why watch over him? He's not going anywhere."

There was a gleam in the logger's eye. He must have been struggling not to smile. Less than five minutes later, everyone was outside, Timar included. They left with an affectation of carelessness, a look of reluctance that was badly put on.

"We're going out for an hour before bed."

"Till tomorrow, Adèle."

Looks were exchanged. The logger touched Timar on the shoulder.

"Come with us. She wants to be alone."

The café was empty. They were six men on the road in the darkness; one of them turned the starter crank of a little truck. The moon shone, the sea murmured—silvery behind the screen of palm trees—just as they had in Timar's imagination when, in Europe, he had tried to picture the tropics.

He turned his head to the café. Its emptiness disconcerted him. The boy was clearing the tables. Adèle was giving him orders from the counter.

Timar noticed that the assistant director of the bank was with them, too. He was jammed against him, standing up, in back of the little truck when they drove off. Already somebody was sighing, "Adèle overdid it. I thought I was going to suffocate before the end of dinner."

"Wait! Stop at my house!" said another, leaning over the driver. "I want to pick up some Pernod."

It was hard to make out the faces, since the moonlight distorted them. The six shadowy figures tried to keep their balance as they were bounced around by all the ruts in the road.

"Where are we going?" Timar asked the assistant director in a low voice.

"To a hut, to spend the evening."

Timar noticed that he looked different than usual. He was a very tall, very thin young man with blond hair and a studied manner. But tonight he seemed suspiciously tense; there was something odd and shifty about his look.

While they were waiting for the Pernod, Timar exchanged a few hushed words with his neighbor. He learned that Bouilloux, who looked like a butcher, had never been a butcher at all but instead a schoolteacher in a village in Morvan.

The banker broke off in the middle of a sentence, in a paroxysm of good manners. He leaned over in the little truck and stuck out his hand.

"Allow me to introduce myself: Gérard Maritain."

"Joseph Timar, of SACOVA."

The vehicle drove off again. Timar didn't know the road they were on, and the noise of the engine made it impossible to talk. Though the truck was little more than a jumble of rusted parts, the driver was speeding, and the passengers were flung together at every turn.

A few lights could be seen on either side, then nothing at all. They made out a fire in the distance. The black cones were native huts.

"To Maria's?" someone asked.

"To Maria's!"

Then Timar was brutally drawn into a nightmare. This was the first time he'd been out at night in Libreville. Everything was unrecognizable under the moon. He didn't know where he was or where he was going.

Shadows gathered about as the truck went by—blacks, no doubt—only to melt back into the jungle. The brakes squealed. Bouilloux got out first, went up to a hut, and kicked the door.

"Maria! Hey, Maria! Get up!"

The others got out in turn. Timar kept close to Maritain, the one who seemed most like him.

"Who's Maria? A prostitute?"

"No, a black like the others. With them, all they want is a white man. There's no bar in Libreville, so tonight we had to . . ."

Even at night it was hot. Nothing stirred in the other huts. The door in front of them opened and the shadowy figure of a naked black came out, waved a greeting, and disappeared into the deeper darkness of the village.

Not until later did Timar realize that this was Maria's husband: you sent him away while you were visiting his wife.

A match flared and an oil lamp lit up in the hut.

"Go on," Bouilloux said. He stepped aside for the others.

Inside it was hotter yet—a cloying, human heat. There was a bitter smell that made Timar gag. He had only had an intimation of it before, when some sweat-soaked blacks had gone by.

With one hand, the woman who'd just lit the oil lamp wrapped a piece of cloth around her naked body. Bouilloux tore it off and threw it in the corner.

"Go get your two sisters! Especially the little one, hey?"

The whites seemed at home in the hut, except for Maritain perhaps. He looked ill at ease. There was a table, two old deck chairs, and a ratty cot that retained the damp impress of human bodies.

Three of the men sat down anyway, after drawing up the covers. "Sit, boys!"

Timar had never been so hot before—not even in the midday sun. The heat seemed unhealthy to him, a feverish heat, the heat of a hospital. He felt physical disgust at the touch of things, at the walls themselves. And he kept looking to Maritain, who was still on his feet, too, though farther inside the hut.

"They're not the equal of Adèle!" Bouilloux shouted out to him.

"Come on, have a drink—it'll do you good."

A glass was passed from hand to hand to Timar, one of three unwashed glasses. Bouilloux and the one-eyed logger had the others.

"To Adèle's health!"

It was straight Pernod. Timar gulped it down because he didn't have the courage to stand up against the others. He drank pinching his nostrils, nauseated by the glass as well as the liquid.

"Very clever to pretend you don't get it. But we've all had her."

Something would have happened then if the door hadn't swung open. Maria came in first, an obliging smile on her lips. Behind her was a very slender young girl. The man nearest to the door grabbed her immediately.

Confusion followed. The hut wasn't big enough for everyone inside. They were all pressed up against each other.

The black women hardly said a thing. Some isolated words and broken phrases. Mostly they laughed—you could see their shining white teeth. Maria took a bottle of crème de menthe from under the mattress and they drained it after the Pernod.

There was a single awkward moment. The one-eyed logger had asked, "What are they saying in the village about Thomas's death?"

The three black faces lost their smiles, their welcoming appearance, even their submissiveness. The women said nothing, staring at the ground. Bouilloux restored the good mood with a loud cry,

"Enough, enough—fuck that dirty black! Cheers, boys! You know what I say we do? Let's go for a ride in the jungle!"

Once again, as at dinner, there was a brief exchange of glances. Timar suspected that Bouilloux's words held a deeper meaning, that they'd hatched a plot.

"Just a moment! Listen, Maria—a hundred francs if you can scare up a bottle of whiskey. Or anything."

She found the whiskey, though there wasn't a sound or light or whisper from the village. Everyone seemed to be asleep. From the huts, you couldn't help but hear what was going on.

Bits and pieces of conversation. They squeezed back onto the truck.

Near the trunk of a kapok tree stood a black woman no one had noticed until then.

"Hey you! Climb in!"

The noise of the starter and the engine made it impossible to hear anything more.

———

Timar didn't want to see a thing. Stubbornly he stared at the passing canopy of moonlit trees. They were driving on sand, and kept having to shift gears all the time.

Someone handed the bottle of whiskey to him, half empty and positively hot, its neck sticky. He couldn't drink. He pretended, though, letting the liquor dribble down his chin and onto his chest.

"*. . . but we've all had her. . .*"

He felt an agonizing impatience. There was only one thought in his head: to confront this animal Bouilloux, to demand an explanation. Because it wasn't true! It wasn't possible! Bouilloux, for example—he'd never been Adèle's lover. Nor the one-eyed man, nor. . .

He alternated between fury and despair. One moment, he imagined ordering them to stop the truck to let him out. But he didn't even know where he was. He didn't have any choice except to see the night through to its end in this company.

He calculated that they'd traveled something like fifteen miles. The truck came to a stop where the road itself ended, at the edge of a clearing by a river. The uproar started again, outbursts of talk and laughter.

"The bottle! Don't forget the bottle!" a shadow yelled out.

Timar remained alone by the little truck. No one noticed. In front of him, he saw figures going back and forth, sometimes zigzagging through the patches of light and shadow. He heard whispers and murmurs, raucous laughter.

Maritain's long shadowy figure was the first to come back. Not expecting it, he discovered Timar when he was only a yard away. Embarrassed, he stammered, "You were here all the time?! A man's got to have fun . . ."

Another shadowy figure—shorter and larger—slipped across the clearing. Suddenly, it came up.

"Quick! Get inside! This is going to be a scream!"

It was Bouilloux. Another shadow turned, then two, three. A black woman came after that.

"Hey, baby, just a second! Whites first!"

They piled into the truck. The three women waited their turn. The engine started up.

"Go!"

The truck sped off as fast as possible. The women were running after it shouting.

"Back, girls, back! Bye-bye!"

They were naked, absolutely naked, like jungle animals. The moon dappled them with silvery light. They were shrieking and waving their arms.

"Faster, faster! They could still catch up!"

The little truck was straining violently. They hit a tree stump and nearly tipped over. It was a close shave.

The black women were still running, but they were gradually

falling behind. Their outlines grew smaller and more distant, their voices fainter.

That was it—they'd lost them!

There were a few giggles, no more, and some stray comments.

"Who was the big fat one?"

Next to Timar, Maritain bowed his head.

A few obscenities, too. But as they drove farther, they fell silent. They became increasingly grim and despondent.

"I have a summons from the chief of police for tomorrow."

"Me, too."

"And Adèle? Speaking of which, we should take up a collection for a wreath."

It was hot and cold. Timar's body was covered in sweat and his shirt was drenched. The air seemed too hot for his lungs and yet the breeze the truck made was freezing him.

He'd started at the sound of Adèle's name. The moon was lower, behind the trees, and he could no longer see his companions. But he knew which corner Bouilloux was sitting in.

"Speaking of Adèle, I want you to tell me . . ."

His voice sounded so false that he was thrown off. He lapsed into silence.

"What do you want to know? Have fun if you want, like we did tonight. Just don't knock her up."

He said nothing. They dropped him off by the edge of the pier. He'd shaken only one hand, Maritain's. Maritain had stammered, "See you tomorrow."

Timar was alone in the night. There was one light shining on the second floor of the hotel. He tried to open the door but it was locked, and he didn't want to make a noise by knocking. There was the dead man, for one thing. He was so jittery that his knees were shaking. He was filled with irrational fear.

He headed around the house to the courtyard door. A stray cat running away made him start. He was shivering even though he was covered in sweat, and it made him wonder if he was falling ill.

The slightest movement made him sweat. He could feel himself sweating and smell himself sweating, could feel every pore of his body spitting out sweat.

The courtyard door was also locked. When he returned to the front, the door swung open.

There was Adèle, a candle in her hand, wearing her usual black silk dress and as calm as ever. There was just room for Timar to slip in the door before it closed behind him again. The candle stopped flickering in the café. He tried to think of something to say. He was appalled, furious at himself, at her, at the whole world. He was more upset than he had ever felt in his life.

"You weren't asleep?"

He looked at her suspiciously and had an unexpected reaction. Was it because of the disgusting displays he'd witnessed that night? Or was it more like an angry protest, a yearning for vengeance?

He gave way, in any case, to a mean, brutal impulse.

"Your new room's on the left."

He followed her like a coward to the stairs they would both have to climb. He knew she'd stop and let him lead the way with the light.

Right then he grabbed her by the waist, but without really knowing what he meant to do.

She didn't struggle. She was still holding the candle, and a drop of hot wax fell onto Timar's hand. She simply pulled away from him. She was a woman, but her torso was muscular and strong— too strong for him to press her to him. All she said was, "You're drunk, my dear. Go get some sleep."

He gave her a troubled look. He saw her pale face in the dancing candlelight and her shapely lips that seemed in spite of everything to be forming a smile that was both ironic and tender.

He hurried awkwardly upstairs, tripped, and went to the wrong door. Without any anger, she said, "It's the door on the left."

After he shut the door, he heard her climbing the stairs. She opened a door and closed it behind her. At last, one after the other, two slippers fell to the floor.

4

AT THE cemetery Timar was overwhelmed by an unexpected wave of emotion. He felt utterly displaced. The feeling washed over him and filled him and left him almost gasping as if he'd been knocked to the ground by a breaker.

Displaced—by the picturesque details, the jaunty palms, the singsong of native speech, the milling black bodies.

But there was something else, too—the clarity and desperation with which he understood that to leave Africa you had to go by boat. There was one every month, and it took three weeks to get to France.

It was eight in the morning. They'd left the Hotel Central at seven to miss the worst of the heat. But the heat wasn't only from the sun: it rose from the ground, the walls, everything. Your own body even gave off heat!

Timar had gone to bed at four. He'd felt sick ever since he got up, which convinced him that he must have been drunker than he'd thought.

The loggers were there, along with Maritain and the rest of the regulars. As in a provincial town, they were stationed in groups several yards from the door. The only difference was that here everyone was dressed in white and that everyone was wearing a sun helmet, even Adèle, who emerged from behind the coffin wearing her black silk dress.

The hearse was the little truck from the night before, now covered in black cloth.

They set out walking along the red dirt road. They turned into a small steep lane lined with native huts. Was one of them Maria's?

In spite of the heat, they walked quickly: if the truck slowed down too much its engine stalled. Adèle took the lead. She was alone and walking quite normally. She looked about and sometimes turned around, like someone in charge.

Finally they reached the cemetery. It was at the top of a hill overlooking the sea and the town. To the left a river flowed out of the jungle. A red-and-black cargo ship was taking on a load of lumber.

Was it because of the purity of the air? In spite of the distance, you could make out the smallest details: some rafts being towed by a very small tugboat with a chugging diesel engine; the clanking chains with which they were securing the stacks of lumber; the creaking cranes.

Farther out was the ocean—ocean and nothing but ocean, three whole weeks of it going full steam ahead before you saw the coast of France!

Was this really a cemetery? There'd been an attempt to respect European tradition. There were two or three stone tombs, a couple of wooden crosses. Even so, it was hardly what you would have expected: no chapel, no enclosing wall, no gate; just a hedge of outlandish shrubbery with monstrous red berries that only underscored how far away Europe was. And the earth was red. Right in the open, at a distance of a hundred yards, you could make out a row of rectangular unmarked mounds—the native graveyard. And in the middle of it, a gigantic baobab tree.

People who hadn't joined in the procession had driven over and were waiting, smoking cigarettes. Among them were the governor and the territorial administrator. They bowed to Adèle.

It had to be done quickly because there was no shade. You could hear the cargo being loaded throughout the ceremony. The pastor was uncomfortable.

In his life, Eugène Renaud had been a Catholic as much as he was anything. But the local curate had left on a tour of the interior several days earlier, and the Anglican pastor had agreed to officiate in his place.

Four blacks slid the coffin into the too-shallow hole. They used hoes to rake the dirt over it.

The idea that one day he might also be interred like this made Timar unbearably conscious of his life since La Rochelle. This wasn't a cemetery! This wasn't a burial! He wasn't at home!

He was sleepy. His stomach ached. He was afraid of the heat that filtered under his helmet and burned his neck like a branding iron.

Everybody headed back to the town. He tried to walk apart, but out of the corner of his eye he saw a figure beside him, the tall figure of Maritain, who mumbled nervously, "Did you sleep well? By the way, have you received a summons, too? It seems that the governor wants to take part in the questioning."

Timar vaguely recognized the market and made out the lane the police station was on. His shirt was sticking to his armpits. He was thirsty.

———

There was no waiting room; they'd made do by setting a couple of chairs out under the veranda. But the glare was so harsh that you couldn't take off your helmet.

The black helpers sat on the wooden steps. The office door remained open and they'd seen the governor and the prosecutor going in. The typewriter clattered away in another office. When it stopped, bits and pieces of conversation came through.

Adèle was the first person they called in. The loggers glanced at one another, especially when they heard the governor's politely deferential voice.

"...unfortunate circumstances... if you'll excuse us... need to clear things up quickly... painful business..."

It lasted barely five minutes. Chairs were pushed back. Adèle came out, not in the least flustered, made her way down the steps, and headed for the hotel. From inside, the police chief cried out, "Next!"

Bouilloux went in, after making a face at his companions. The typewriter clattered. Nothing could be heard. The logger came out. He gave a shrug.

"Next!"

Timar, the last in line, hesitated to ask a black for a glass of water.

"She was the governor's mistress," whispered Maritain in his ear. "That's what makes the whole business so complicated."

Timar didn't answer, but instead moved up a place when it was the assistant director's turn to be called into the office.

"...certain no one left the room between midnight and four? ...Thank you..."

The chief of police followed Maritain to the door, glanced around the veranda, and spotted Timar.

"You've been here all along? Come in, then!"

His round face was shiny with sweat. Timar followed him into the room where, because of the contrast with the light outside, he could see nothing but shadows among shadows. An indistinct figure was sitting with knees parted next to a side table covered with glasses.

"This, Mr. Governor, is Mr. Timar, about whom I was just telling you."

The governor stuck out a moist hand.

"Pleased to meet you. Have a seat...Can you believe it? My wife is from Cognac, too. She knew your uncle very well."

And, turning to a third person, "Mr. Joseph Timar, a young man of excellent family...Mr. Pollet, our prosecutor. Do you have another glass, Chief?"

Timar had to get used to the dimness and stripes of light from the blinds. The police chief poured the whiskey and operated the siphon.

"Whatever gave you the idea to come to Gabon?"

The governor was some sixty years old, large and red-faced. His white hair stood out in sharp contrast to his blotchy red skin, but it lent him a distinguished air, and he was friendly in the way that men of a certain age are when they enjoy some power—and enjoy eating and drinking even better.

"Oh, not SACOVA! Are you aware that if it hadn't been for our renegotiating the fines they'd run up, the company would be bankrupt by now?"

"I wasn't aware of it. My uncle—"

"Is he ever going to run for the senate?"

"I think so, yes."

"Cheers! You must have a fine opinion of Libreville! Sometimes we can go for two years without an incident, and then the scandals rain down. Why, just last night it seems a bunch of hoodlums abandoned some women out in the jungle. That hasn't made my job any easier, with the blacks furious about Thomas's murder."

The prosecutor was much younger. Timar had seen him before, on the day of the party, drinking with the Englishmen.

"Chief, any questions for him?"

"Not especially. I've already taken the liberty of issuing him a summons. That's how we first met. By the way, Mr. Timar, if you intend to stay on at the hotel, I suggest a degree of prudence. The inquiry has revealed certain facts to us…"

He waited before going on, but the governor continued good-naturedly, judging Timar worthy of hearing everything. "Apparently, it was that woman who killed Thomas—we have proof of it, almost enough to take to court. We recovered the bullet casing. It's the same caliber as the Renauds' pistol."

He held out his box of cigars.

"Don't smoke? It's most inconvenient that she's the one, but we can't do anything about it, and we need to set an example this time. You understand? She'll be watched. Her every movement will be observed. If she makes just one mistake…"

"What I wonder," murmured the prosecutor, who'd said nothing as yet, "is what the boy could have done to her. This isn't a woman to just snap. She knows how to take care of herself."

Timar would have preferred to be questioned like the others, in a dry tone, standing before the desk.

Why was everyone so stubbornly interested in him? Why were they so set on finding a place for him in town, even the authorities, who had now admitted him into their circle and their secrets?

"Of course, you know nothing about it, do you? The loggers are sticking together. Not one will talk, and that's natural. Any other time and we probably could have hushed the whole thing up. You didn't see anyone leave in the course of the night?"

"No."

"You'll have to come to our house for dinner one of these evenings. My wife will be delighted to meet you. And don't forget that we have a club, a very modest club, just across from the pier. It's better than nothing. Anytime you feel like a couple of hands of bridge…"

He rose, putting an end to the meeting with the ease of a man used to conducting official business.

"Good-bye, my dear friend. If there's anything at all I can do for you, don't hesitate to ask."

Timar saluted awkwardly, with a slightly excessive degree of ceremony. Outside he saw the sea again, flat as a pond, and the image that had haunted him that morning came back. It was a map of France, a tiny little France right at the edge of the ocean, the familiar map with its rivers, its administrative regions whose shape he knew by heart, its towns. The governor was from Le Havre, his wife from Cognac. One of the loggers came from Limoges, another from Poitiers. Bouilloux had been born in the Morvan.

They were all neighbors. Timar, in La Rochelle, could have visited every one of them in a couple of hours. And they were gathered here, a mere handful of them, on a narrow strip of land carved out of the equatorial jungle. Boats came and went, little boats like the one he'd seen this morning, with flies buzzing around the winches. And up there, overlooking Libreville, was the cemetery— a fake.

Timar passed the SACOVA building, spotted the director in the back, behind a counter crowded with black women. They greeted each other with a wave of the hand.

At that point it wasn't just the misery of homesickness that had him in its grip: it was a sense of futility. The futility of being here! The futility of struggling against the sun that penetrated his every pore. The futility of the quinine that lifted his spirits and that he swallowed every night. The futility of living and dying, only to be buried in a fake cemetery by four half-naked blacks.

"Whatever made you want to come to Gabon?" the governor had asked.

What about him? What about all the others? What about that SACOVA employee, up there in the middle of the jungle, who threatened to shoot anyone who came to take his place?

It was August. In La Rochelle, near the harbor entrance, on the beach with its border of salt cedar, young men and girls were lying on the sand.

"Timar? He went off to Gabon."

"Lucky bastard! What an adventure!"

Because that's how they'd talk. While he was just sitting here, his legs weak, in a countryside that was the color of rust. The idea of going back flitted through his head, but he rejected it outright.

True, he was the nephew of Gaston Timar, counselor general and future senator. But what he hadn't said was that his father worked for the town council, that he'd had to leave the university for lack of funds, that he didn't even have enough money to go out with his friends to a café or nightclub.

The flatboat that was supposed to take him to his post in the interior was still lying on the sand among the native canoes. Nobody was working on it; nobody was worrying about repairing it.

Suddenly—and so abruptly that he startled himself—Timar made a decision. Gasping at his own audacity, he carried it out. A garage where they repaired cars, machines, and boats faced the sea. He went in. A white man was trying to start up an old car by getting some blacks to push it.

"Could you fix that boat there?"

"Who's paying for it—SACOVA?" The man waved his finger to show he wouldn't do it.

"No. I'll pay."

"That's different. You realize it could run to several thousand francs."

An obscure force was driving Timar on, a need for action, for heroism. He opened his wallet.

"Here's a down payment of a thousand. It's urgent."

"All I need is three days. Something to drink?"

So the die was cast! In three days, the flatboat would be repaired and Timar would head off to take over his post. That would be a real feat.

Timar opened the door to the hotel with a firm, categoric movement. The big room was empty, bathed in the familiar shadow of African houses. The tables had already been set for lunch. Adèle was alone behind the counter.

Before he even sat down, Timar announced, "I leave in three days." He wasn't looking at her.

"For Europe?"

"No. The interior."

The word, which was so nice to utter, brought Adèle's ambiguous smile to her lips. Annoyed, Timar went off to sit in the corner and pretend to read newspapers he'd read twice already. She didn't pay him any attention. She came and went, gave orders to the kitchen, rearranged bottles, opened up the till.

He was furious. He needed to stir things up. From the very first word he knew he was making a mistake, but it was too late to stop.

"You know they found the bullet casing?"

"Ah."

"The casing of the bullet that killed Thomas."

"I understood the first time."

"That's all you have to say?"

She turned her back to him and arranged the bottles.

"What do you want me to say?"

They exchanged words across the empty damp room with its bands of light and shadow.

"You should watch out."

He didn't mean to threaten her. Still, he would have liked to give her a bit of a scare.

"Emile!"

Her only response was to call for the boy. He came running.

"Put these carafes of wine on the tables."

The boy kept darting in and out between them after that, making his way from one table to another. The raw white of his waiter's outfit was like a stain.

The loggers showed up, then Maritain, as well as a notary clerk, and a traveling salesman from England, and the atmosphere was just like every other meal, though this time the events of the previous night led to murmurs and stifled laughter.

Timar's bleary-eyed face was the most haggard of the lot.

———

That night, he remained in his corner until the very last moment, pretending to read. Maritain had left first. The loggers had gone on playing card games with the clerk until ten, when they all trooped off heavily. The boy had locked the doors, closed the windows and blinds, and turned out some of the lights. Timar still hadn't spoken a word to Adèle. He hadn't even looked at her.

But now that the doors and windows were shut, he was relishing the intimacy.

She was at the counter, locking up the drawers with a key. Had she guessed his thoughts? Had she been looking at him? Had she glanced at him sometimes in the course of the evening?

He heard the boy declare, "All done, ma'am!"

"Good. Get to bed."

She lit a candle, because the electric generator would soon cut off.

Timar stood up, uncertain, and approached the counter. When he was almost there, Adèle headed for the door and the staircase, candle in hand.

"Coming?"

All he could do was follow. She climbed in front of him and he saw her naked legs, the dress that spread like a corolla. She stopped on the landing, and he stammered, "Which room do I . . ."

"Your old one, of course."

The one he'd slept in the first few days, the one where she'd come to him one morning, the one he'd been exiled from so they could put the coffin in there. She was handing him the candle. He realized clearly that, when he took it, it would be all over. She'd go to her own room. He'd have to go off to his bed. That was why he remained standing, awkward, hesitant. She jiggled the candle in her hand as a sign for him to take it.

"Adèle!"

It was hard to go on. He didn't know what he wanted. He was like a little boy whining for no reason, or simply because he's unhappy—unhappy about everything and nothing.

Adèle was half in shadow. There was a hint of a smile as she took the two steps to Timar's door and opened it. She let him in first, then closed the door behind her and set the candle on the dresser.

"What do you want?"

Maybe it was the light that made her body stand out so clearly under her dress, its blackness tinged with red.

"I want . . ."

He stretched out his hands the way he had the night before. He touched her, but he was afraid to take her in his arms. She didn't push him away. She barely moved.

"See, you're not going to be leaving in three days. Get in bed."

She spoke and pulled off her dress. She opened the mosquito net, smoothed the sheets, and fluffed the pillows. After stripping to the waist, he paused.

She got in the bed ahead of him, as if they'd always slept together there. She waited without impatience.

"Blow out the candle."

5

HE FELT better when he woke up. Before he even opened his eyes, he could tell that the bed beside him was empty. He felt around with his hand and smiled, straining to hear the sounds of the house. The boy was sweeping the big room. Adèle must be behind the counter. He rose lazily, and his first thought looking out the window was: "It's going to rain."

Just like Europe! And just as he used to in Europe, he frowned for an instant at the thought of having to carry an umbrella. The low sky was a solid dark gray. The downpour seemed to be only minutes away, but the soft, hot radiance of the missing sun was still palpable. It wasn't going to rain. It wasn't going to rain for another six months—Timar was in Gabon. The thought made him smile with resignation, but a little aggressively, too, as he reached for the pitcher.

He hadn't slept well. Several times, half awake, he'd opened his eyes a little and seen the milky form of the woman beside him, against him, her head resting on one bent arm.

Had Adèle slept? Twice she'd made him shift position; he'd been lying on his right side and having trouble breathing. When he'd opened his eyes yet again it was daylight. Adèle was standing by the door, looking for hairpins she might have dropped during the night.

Timar blew his nose and wiped it. He looked at his tired face in the mirror. Something was bothering him, but he didn't want to think about it because he was too inexperienced with women to solve it. Last night Adèle had given herself for sure, but somehow it seemed like she'd given too much. She'd done it for him, not for herself.

He was almost certain she hadn't slept or even closed her eyes, that she'd spent the whole night against him, her head resting on her folded arm, staring straight ahead into blackness. What was that about?

Timar was sick of worrying. He'd come to a decision as he washed: leave it to chance and let things turn out the way they would.

He went downstairs and realized that the heavy sky was making it even hotter. After taking a few steps he was sweating. He pushed open the door to the café. Adèle was there, behind the counter, the tip of a pencil between her lips. He didn't know what to do, so he stuck out his hand.

"Good morning."

She batted her eyelashes in reply. Then, licking the point of her pencil, she returned to her accounts.

"Boy! Mr. Timar's breakfast!"

Twice he caught her studying him, but perhaps she wasn't aware of it herself.

"Not too tired?"

"I'm okay."

She shut the register, put away the papers on the counter, and came to sit at the table where Timar was eating. It was the first time she'd done anything like that. Before speaking, she looked him over once again. There was a hint of indecision in her eyes.

"Are you on very good terms with your uncle?"

That was about the most unexpected thing she could have said! So she was also interested in his famous uncle?

"Yes, very good. He's my godfather—I went to say my farewells before I left."

"Is he on the right or left?"

"He belongs to a party called the Popular Democrats—something like that."

"I suppose you know that SACOVA is bankrupt, or close to it."

Stunned, Timar drank his coffee. He wondered if he'd really slept with this woman who was now carefully weighing her every word. But then was she so different from the Adèle he'd taken in his arms?

———

This was when the atmosphere of the house was somehow at its most intimate—cleaning time, the time for small domestic tasks. You could make out the low hum of the native market even though it was some four hundred yards away. Women walked by, their waists draped with cloth, carrying jars or food wrapped in banana leaves on their heads.

Adèle was pale. Her skin must have always been like that—matte, even-toned, smooth. It looked like it had never been touched by the sun. Did she have the same finely creased eyelids when she was younger?

When Timar was six, he'd experienced a great love—the memory still haunted him. It had been his teacher. At the time he lived in a village where the children were all taught together until high school.

Like Adèle, the teacher always dressed in black, and her expression was a similar mix of severity and tenderness. Above all, she displayed the same calm, so alien to Timar's character.

Right now, for instance, he wanted to take Adèle's hand in his, to say silly things, to whisper reminiscences of the night before. But seeing her with the face of a schoolteacher grading homework, he grew confused and blushed. And yet he wanted her more than ever.

"So you see, there's a good chance you'll return to France empty-handed."

What she was saying should have grated on him, or been hateful. And yet somehow she managed to make her words almost soothing. She enveloped him in a tenderness all of her own, something that went beyond her actions or words.

The boy was polishing the brass bar. Adèle was contemplating Timar's forehead as if it was far, far away.

"On the other hand, there's a way to make a million in three years."

Once again, if anyone else had said that, he would have found it intolerable. Now she stood up. She was speaking even more carefully, pacing back and forth across the café. The sound of her high heels on the flagstones gave rhythm to her sentences. Each one stood out, followed by the exact same silence. Adèle's smile suited her strange voice. Maybe it seemed low class to some people, but it was full of personality, sometimes soft, sometimes shrill like cheap music.

What was she saying? It blended in with his other impressions: the black women still filing past outside, the skinny, nervous legs of the boy in his white shorts, the panting of a diesel engine someone somewhere was trying to adjust. And then there were the images her own words evoked. She mentioned loggers and instantly he saw Bouilloux's face lit by the oil lamp in Maria's hut.

"They don't buy the land—the government gives them a three-year concession."

Why, as he gazed at her, did he see her again the way she'd looked that morning, searching for her hairpins while he pretended to sleep?

She pulled a bottle from a shelf, set two glasses on the table, and filled them with calvados. Was she from Normandy? It was the third time he'd seen her drink apple brandy.

"The first colonists were given concessions for thirty years or more—even a perpetual lease."

A perpetual lease—the words stuck with him for a long time as she went on talking. He kept trying to think what they reminded him of.

"In principle. Usually the rights revert to the state when the settler dies, but—"

She never wore stockings or underwear and he had seldom seen such white legs. He looked at them because he knew Adèle was looking at him. She seemed to be trying make up her mind about something once and for all.

A black came in and laid some fish on the counter.

"That's fine! I'll pay you next time."

She drank the liquor like a medicine, making a face as she swallowed.

"There's a guy called Truffaut who's been here for twenty-eight years and gone native. He married a black woman and has ten or twelve children with her. He's furious because now that they have boats with outboard motors his concession is only a day's journey from Libreville."

Their eyes met. Timar knew that she was perfectly aware he wasn't listening, but there was only a flicker of impatience on her face. Unperturbed, she went on, just like his old teacher, who'd continue her lesson to the end even when the children weren't paying attention in the least.

The situation was the same—the same sense of distraction, the same desire to be doing something else, the same resignation. In his mind, Timar pictured Truffaut as a biblical patriarch among his children of color.

"With a hundred thousand francs..."

And he saw himself giving the first thousand of the three thousand francs to the mechanic, who at that very moment was busy repairing the flatboat.

"His oldest son would like to study in Europe."

Adèle's hand lay on top of his. She seemed to be asking for a moment, just one moment, of serious attention.

"I can supply the money. And you, you'll supply your uncle's support. The Minister of Colonies is a member of the same party. Your uncle can see to it that we're awarded an exemption, and..."

When he looked at her again, she was licking the point of her pencil, as she had at the counter; then she wrote out laboriously:

SACOVA POSITION BAD. STOP. RISK NOT HAVING JOB. STOP. HAVE FOUND OPPORTUNITY WITH BRILLIANT

FUTURE. STOP. NECESSARY YOU SEE COLONIES MINISTER IN PARIS AND OBTAIN SPECIAL AUTHORIZATION FOR CESSION TO ME OF TRUFFAUT PERPETUAL LEASE. STOP. ALL URGENCY REQUIRED AS INFORMATION MAY BECOME KNOWN. STOP. HAVE SECURED CAPITAL FOR EXPLOITA-TION OF CLAIM AND COUNT ON YOUR KINDNESS FOR STEPS THAT WILL MAKE MY FORTUNE. STOP. MUCH LOVE.

Timar smiled at the final words. Adèle could hardly know that in his family men weren't especially demonstrative. Certainly no one would take such a familiar tone with Timar's uncle.

The whole time she was writing, he'd been conscious of his superiority to her. He'd even smiled with a tender condescension of his own. Her way of holding herself, of licking the point of her pencil, of spelling out her words with too much care, all betrayed her lack of education and her social class.

"Is that pretty much what you'd have written?"

"More or less, yes. I'd change a word or two."

"Well, do it!"

And she went back to her counter, where she had something to do. When she returned, he was reading over his revision of the telegram, not quite believing it. Later, he'd be incapable of saying just when the decision had been reached. Had there even been a decision? At any rate, just before noon the boy took the telegram to the post office, and it had been Adèle who, without thinking twice, had taken the money for it from the cash register.

"Now, here's some advice—go pay the governor a visit."

Timar hadn't been out all day. He jumped at the chance, but not at the idea of going to see the governor. He changed his shirt anyway, since his was soaked through.

———

The town was even more depressing than usual because of the yellowish-green light and the oppressive heat, something that seemed inexplicable since there was no sun overhead. Timar noticed that even the blacks at the market were sweating heavily.

You waited without thinking for a clap of thunder for days, but no—there were going to be days and weeks of this draining atmosphere before a storm broke, days and weeks without rain or a trickle of water. And you were afraid even to remove your sun helmet to wipe off your forehead!

Timar meant to pass the governor's house looking the other way when the chief of police hailed him from the top of the steps.

"Coming in?"

"What about you?"

"I'm just leaving. But go have a whiskey with the governor. It'll please him; he's told me a lot about you."

In spite of the oppressive humidity, things were happening fast, too fast. Timar found himself in a large drawing room exactly like a prefect's back in La Rochelle, Nantes, or Moulins. Some leopard skins added an exotic note and clashed with the tapestries and carpets from the rue du Sentier.

"Ah! It's you, young man!"

The governor's wife was summoned, a woman of about forty who wasn't ugly or pretty. A woman trained to make tea and listen to men talk.

"You're from La Rochelle? You must know my brother-in-law, the departmental archivist."

"He's your brother-in-law?"

Whiskey. The governor sat with his knees slightly apart. He exchanged a look with his wife. Timar understood why the governor was glad to have company. He liked to drink. His wife didn't like him to. When he had a guest, he kept filling his guest's glass so he could fill his own, too.

"Cheers! So, what are you going to do? SACOVA is getting worse and worse. I'll tell you this in confidence, but . . ."

Their chat lasted a quarter of an hour. Not a word about the murdered black or the investigation. Once again Timar's head was thick with drink before lunch. He liked the feeling: his thoughts floated free, avoiding the rough edges.

At the hotel, they looked at him with distinct curiosity—probably because he'd had a drink with the governor. The loggers were in the middle of a conversation: "...so I gave him the hundred francs and a kick in the ass, and he left, happy as can be..."

Timar soon realized they were talking about the tail end of the night in the forest. Maria's husband had shown up, making a fuss —he'd even threatened to hire someone to write to the League of Nations. A hundred francs and a kick in the ass! Everyone handed over twenty francs, except Timar. They were afraid to ask him.

He napped until five and came back downstairs feeling queasy. Two glasses of whiskey restored him.

"Did the governor have anything to say?"

"Nothing of interest."

"I sent a black to tell Truffaut we're ready to make a deal."

"But we don't know yet if—"

"We can send him back home if it doesn't work out."

He looked at her in alarm. And yet she was a woman, a real woman—with soft skin, a good figure, a yielding body.

Just before dinner he walked to the water to check out his half-repaired boat.

"You can leave in two days," the mechanic told him.

Dusk was subdued, the sea and the sky a poisonous green. Lights came on. Dinner. Billiards and card games with the loggers and the notary clerk with the enormous gut.

Maritain asked Timar, "Do you play chess?"

"Yes...no...not today."

"Have you come down with something?"

"I don't know."

He felt bad all over; he didn't know what to do with himself. He didn't feel at home anywhere, and he wondered what was going to happen with Adèle that night.

Would they simply end up in the same room and sleep in the same bed? The whole thing was starting to feel routine, and that horrified Timar, especially since her husband, Eugène, had been sleeping in the same bed only four days ago.

But he suffered when he didn't see Adèle. He suffered when one of customers called her by her first name.

Finally, what he needed was an explanation from her. About Thomas. He absolutely had to have it, and yet he was afraid to ask. Had she killed the black man? He was almost sure of it. It didn't bother him all that much, he just wanted to know how and why. And he wanted to know the reason for her being so tranquil.

The café was lighted by four electric bulbs. It was filled with the clack of billiard balls and the voices of cardplayers, and it seemed like any provincial café. Timar downed two more drinks, then took advantage of a moment when Adèle was away serving someone to head for the stairs. "I'm off to bed. Good night!"

She lifted her head. He caught a mere glimpse of her terrible smile, half ironic and half tender. She was laughing at him. She knew he was running away, and she knew why. And it didn't worry her.

He hadn't expected to sleep soundly, but he did, and when he woke up it was already day. Adèle was standing beside his bed in her black dress.

"Feeling any better?"

"But..."

How did she know he'd been feeling sick? She sat on the edge of the bed as she had the first time, when Eugène and Thomas were still alive. He let his hand stray over to her dress and slowly pulled her close. It was quick, mainly because of the sensation of cold, naked flesh—Adèle had just showered—underneath the soft silk.

"I have to go downstairs."

He waited two hours before following her. He puttered around, looking through the little things his mother and his sister had packed for him, odd useless things like a thimble and an assortment of different-colored spools of thread: "You'll have to mend your clothes on your own over there."

There was even a selection of buttons—the two women must have scoured every sewing shop in La Rochelle. Timar could almost hear them saying, "It's for my son. He's leaving for Gabon next week. There won't be any women over there to . . ."

He went down and ate, exchanging only a few words with Adèle. He announced he'd be stopping by the chief of police.

"Good idea," she said.

He went, in fact. He was served the customary glass of whiskey.

"What's new with you? Are people asking why the investigation's stalled?"

"I haven't heard anything in particular."

"Thomas's father came in from the bush. A native clerk who worked for a lawyer for two years has taken him under his wing. He's getting pushy—claiming I don't know how much in damages. By the way, has the hotel manager found a new man?"

"I don't know."

"That's plain to see. You, you could live here for twenty years without even suspecting the kinds of things that go on!"

Lunch. A stupefying snooze. Cocktail. Dinner. Once again Timar left before closing time. He didn't sleep. He heard all the conversations, the sound of the billiard balls, the coins jingling on the counter, the boy shutting the venetian blinds and locking the doors. At last Adèle, on her way up. He hesitated, couldn't bring himself to get out of bed, and spent two solid hours trying to fall asleep between the clammy sheets.

At ten in the morning he was still sleeping when the door burst open. Adèle came in, excited as can be, a piece of paper in her outstretched right hand.

"Your uncle's reply! Read it, quickly!"

He unsealed the telegram without quite realizing what he was doing. The dateline was Paris.

TRUFFAUT CONCESSION EASILY GRANTED. STOP. ADVISE EXTREME CAUTION WITH REGARD TO PARTNERSHIPS AND SOURCES OF CAPITAL. STOP. PLEASE CONSULT LIBREVILLE NOTARY AND SIGN NOTHING WITHOUT APPROVAL. STOP. WISH YOU ALL FUTURE SUCCESS. STOP. GASTON TIMAR.

Timar didn't know if he was pleased, furious, or worried. But he noticed something new. Until then, Adèle had treated him with a degree of condescension. Now, however, she was looking at him admiringly. Finally she was showing some emotion. She gazed at him fondly and suddenly kissed him on both cheeks.

"Well, you're someone—there's no denying it!"

She went on glibly, handing him his clothes.

"Old man Truffaut's downstairs. He's good for a hundred thousand, with a case or two of whiskey thrown in. Look—you've got another bite."

She touched her finger to Timar's chest, just below the right breast, the way she'd done once before.

"You have a woman's skin! I'm going to call the notary and set up a meeting."

She went out. It was the first time she'd been so excited. Timar rose, with a heavy glance at his surroundings. Glasses clinked below—no doubt she was plying old Truffaut with drink.

"*. . . extreme caution . . . sources of capital . . .*"

He cut himself shaving, looked around without success for his alum, and went downstairs with a streak of blood on his cheek. He was expecting to find a grimy, bearded backwoodsman. Instead a little wizened old man, neatly dressed in a starched suit, got up to greet him.

"It seems it's you who . . ."

Was Timar too nervous? Was it the streak of blood zigzagging down to his chin, or perhaps just the glare, stronger that morning than usual? He found himself overcome by a sense of panic that he'd experienced two or three times since he'd been in Libreville, at noon, among others, on that red dirt path, when he'd felt like his sun helmet was too tight and that if he didn't escape from under the sun right away it would crush him. His vision grew hazy. Things began to wobble, just a bit, the way they do when you look at them through the steam from a boiling pot.

He was on his feet, facing the little old man who was waiting to take his seat again, and Adèle, her elbows on the counter, was watching them both with an almost animal satisfaction. Standing on a chair, the boy was winding the clock.

Timar sat down. He ran his hand across his forehead and rested his elbows on the table.

"Adèle—a whiskey!"

He was struck by that; it was the first time he'd called her by her name in the café, saying it out loud, in the same tone of voice and just as naturally as one of the loggers or the notary clerk.

6

"Happy?" she asked him, gazing into his eyes with her chin on her folded hands.

"Yes," he said, draining his glass of champagne.

"We'll be there soon."

She spoke slowly, watching him, and Timar had the disagreeable impression that he was being tested.

"Is it my fault we're not there already?" he asked irritably.

"Be nice, Joe. I never said it was."

He'd grown morbidly touchy. He was depressed. You could see it in his haggard features, his feverish eyes, his abnormal and shifty glance.

"Everything all right, children?" the owner came over to ask. That night, he was dressed in the white uniform of a cook.

Because from now on the owner of the Central was Bouilloux, the ex-logger and cleaner of Libreville's drains. They'd struck a deal just like that, amid laughter, on one of the first nights after it became known that Timar and Adèle had a concession in the interior. The card game was dragging on. Adèle was going over her accounts. In the middle of a hand, Bouilloux had asked, "So, who's going to take over this place now?"

"I haven't thought about it yet."

"How much are you asking for it?"

"What do you care? You're too poor no matter what."

They joked around. Bouilloux came up to the counter.

"Maybe we could work something out. I've never owned a bar, but I think I could pull it off."

"Let's talk about it again tomorrow morning."

The next day it was done. Bouilloux handed over fifty thousand francs in cash and signed some papers to make up the balance.

That had been three weeks ago, but this was the first night that the café was actually his. Wearing his cook's uniform, he offered champagne all around. And for the first time since the death of Eugène Renaud, the gramophone was playing. Several residents of Libreville had joined the regulars.

Timar and Adèle sat across from each other at a little table and didn't speak much. Every few minutes Adèle looked at her companion intently. His brow was furrowed with worry.

He wasn't sick, simply tired. The strange month he'd just lived through had been filled with events that had come so rapidly and been so unsettling that he still hadn't grasped their import.

He had barely gotten to Libreville before he found himself in an office with Adèle seated next to a notary and using her finger to point out the various deletions and corrections that should be made. The concession was in Timar's name, but there was a binding contract between him and the widow Renaud, who brought two hundred thousand francs to the deal, a hundred thousand for the concession and the rest for improvements to the land. Every foreseeable event had been accounted for, everything was in order, and Timar, who didn't have any objections, signed the papers he was handed one by one.

There had been a lot of details to attend to after that, but the main thing was he'd settled into a routine that had become absolutely indispensable to him. There was, for instance, the walk down the esplanade along the red path with its border of palms. Timar always stopped at a fixed time at the market, then at the place where the native canoes landed their fish, at last at the pier across from the governor's house.

The heat made the walk oppressive, and yet he took it every day, as if it were a duty, and each day he asked himself where he was going to stop for a whiskey. Most often it was at the police chief's. He sat down and said, "Don't let me interrupt your work."

"I'm done. What's new? A whiskey?"

They chatted in the warm shade of the office. This lasted until the day the citizens of Libreville learned about the concession and the partnership between Timar and Adèle. Suddenly, the police chief was a changed man. He seemed put out. He puffed away at his pipe, looking at the bands of shadow and light.

"You know that the investigation is still continuing and that our opinion remains unchanged. I'll tell you the truth: All we're missing is the pistol. Adèle has stashed it away. But no matter— one of these days..."

And the chief of police got up and walked across the room.

"Perhaps you made an unwise move. You, a young man with the brightest of futures..."

Timar's response never varied. With a trace of a smile, ironic and condescending, he rose to collect his sun helmet.

"Let's drop it, all right?"

He left, looking very dignified, and maintained the attitude for as long as he thought he was being watched. He wanted it to seem like he knew what he was doing.

The most logical thing, now that he was on the other side, would have been to avoid the three individuals who represented the enemy camp: the governor, the chief of police, and the prosecutor. Some confused instinct, hope or a wish to show off, drove him to visit all three.

With the prosecutor it was simple enough. His host served him three whiskies, one after the other, and gave him an earful.

"You, my friend, are about to take a bath. It's none of my business. But still, try to get out before it's too late. Adèle is a pretty girl. In bed, she's something else. But afterward, that's it. Understood?"

And Timar found himself on the veranda wearing his knowing look.

At the governor's, by contrast, the blow had been brutal. While

Timar waited in the anteroom, the boy went into the office he knew so well. Timar heard the governor say, without lowering his voice, "Tell the gentleman I'm very busy. I don't know when I'll have any time to see him."

Timar's ears reddened, but he didn't move a muscle. Even when there was no one around to see, he'd trained himself to wear his cynical smile.

He went back the way he came—following the esplanade until he reached the shadowy hotel, with Adèle at the register and the regulars. He went on pretending he was just another guest, having his meals with the others. Downstairs, there was never any intimacy between Adèle and him. Just like Bouilloux or the one-eyed man, he'd shout, "Adèle! A Pernod!"

Because he'd learned to drink Pernod. He'd picked up some other habits, too, and almost made them into rituals. At noon, for instance, before everyone sat down to eat, they played a game of cards at the bar. The loser paid for the round. At night, right after dinner, they arranged for a couple of games of belote. Timar was an avid participant. From time to time, someone or another would cry out, "Adèle! Another round!"

And he was mastering an entirely new vocabulary. The others would sometimes look at each other as if to say, "He's making progress."

And yet it depressed Timar, too, seeing himself there in the crushing heat, with cards in hand for hours on end, his blood thickened by alcohol. He turned moody then. He'd take exception to the slightest thing, a single word, a look.

In short, he was no longer one of the enemy. He had nothing to do with officials or sober types. And yet twenty years of this still wasn't going to make him one of the loggers, or like the notary clerk with the big gut, who played cards using a whole set of words that Timar had never heard before.

The doors and shutters were locked. Adèle went up first, candle in hand, and the electric generator shut down. On the landing, a moment of hesitation—this was a daily occurrence. Adèle turned to look at her companion. Some days he'd say, "Good night."

And she'd say the same, handing him the candle before she went to her room without a kiss or a touch of the hand.

Other times, he murmured, "Come."

Though it was no more than a movement of the lips, she understood. Without a trace of self-consciousness she entered his room, placed the candle on the dresser, opened the mosquito net, and readied the bed before getting in and waiting for him.

"Tired?"

"Not at all."

He didn't want to be tired, but in fact—even though he didn't work and never had to make an effort of any sort—he could barely stand. His exhaustion must have been due to a weakening of his blood. The main symptoms were the hollowness in his head and the shapeless anxiety that sometimes made him shake with terror.

And the worse he felt, the more furiously and passionately he threw himself on Adèle. When he gripped her in his embrace, he asked himself questions that had no answers. Did he love her? What sort of love could she feel for him? Was he wronging her? Would he wrong her one of these days? Why had she killed Thomas? Why...

He didn't ask Adèle any questions. He didn't dare. He was afraid of her answers. He was crazy about her. When he wandered along the esplanade, he'd think about her naked body under her dress and he was filled with hatred for other men.

What really disturbed him was her gaze. For a while now, she'd been watching him, and it was too much! Even in the darkness of the room, holding her in his arms, he could feel her eyes fixed on the white blur of his face. She watched him during meals from the counter where she sat. She watched him when he was playing belote or cards. And there was a judgment to her look, an indulgent one perhaps, but a judgment for all that.

What did she think of him? That was what he wanted to know.

"You shouldn't drink Pernod. It doesn't do you any good."

But he drank it anyway. Because he was wrong and she was right!

They'd had to wait for official papers to come from Paris before all the legal formalities could be concluded. The papers had arrived by boat five days earlier. Timar hadn't wanted to go down to the pier to get them. From his room he'd spotted the steamship from France pulling into the outer harbor. He'd followed the course of the launch as it made its way to the shore.

"Since the hotel has been sold, there's nothing to keep us from leaving as soon as tomorrow," Adèle had said. "Just a day by flatboat and we'll be at the concession."

But they hadn't left that day, or the day after, because Timar had thrown up difficulties, always finding an excuse, always slowing down the preparations.

***

He was furious. Adèle's eyes were fixed on him and he knew all too well what she was thinking. She thought he was scared, that now that it was time to leave Libreville he'd fallen prey to irrational panic, that he was hanging on to the little habits that had become his whole life. It was true. The café—which had seemed so hostile to begin with, which he had hated so much—he looked at it now through different eyes. He knew every last detail. Silly things seemed touching to him, like the native mask that hung on the pearl-gray wall. The mask was a glaring white. The wall had been whitewashed. The relationship between the two tones was remarkably fine and delicate.

Only the polished brass bar made him feel safe, since it was just like the ones in any provincial café in France, with the same bottles, the same aperitifs and liqueurs.

He was safe, but only for the length of his morning walk, when he'd pass through the market and pause for a moment to watch the fishermen pulling their boats onto the sand.

Conversation went on humming around their table in the café. From time to time Adèle, motionless, replied to someone's question. She had her elbows on the table and her chin in her hands, and she was keeping a close watch on Timar, who was going through cigarette after cigarette, angrily puffing out clouds of smoke.

"Have you already got a load for the German cargo ship that comes in next month?"

"Maybe," Adèle would say.

And she waved away the cloud of smoke that lay like a smudge over Timar's face.

Bouilloux joked around, accentuating the grotesqueness of his foot-high white toque. He'd decked it out with a tricolored cockade.

"Allow me, dear friend, to pour you a glass of ambrosia. And how much does it cost me, this ambrosia? When I was a customer, I paid eighty francs a bottle. But now?"

Everyone laughed. Bouilloux, encouraged, thought he'd risk something obscene.

"Will madame be sleeping here tonight? With this young man? Boy, escort the prince and princess to their hall of mirrors!"

Timar was the only one who didn't laugh. And yet his discomfort was physical instead of moral, as if he'd taken a breath of polluted air. Sweat streamed down his forehead. He'd noticed that he sweated more than the others did, and he was ashamed of it. It seemed like a defect. Sometimes Adèle leaned over him in bed and wiped his chest off with a towel.

"How hot you are!"

Her body was hot, too, but the heat didn't have the same intensity to it. And her skin was always smooth.

"You'll see—you'll get used to it. When we're there . . ."

"There" was deep in the jungle, but it wasn't the jungle that scared him. Since he'd been in Libreville, he'd learned that wild animals didn't attack men, especially not white men; that fewer people died of snakebites than from being hit by lightning; and that the blacks out in the brush, the savage-looking ones, were actually the most docile of the lot.

Leopards, elephants, gorillas, gazelles, and crocodiles: every day, or nearly every day, hunters came in with their skins. Even the insects, the tsetse flies he had seen in the town, no longer terrified him much, and when he gave a start, it was purely instinctive.

No, he wasn't scared. It was just that he was being forced to leave Libreville, the hotel, the room with its bands of light and shadow, the red earth of the esplanade, the sea edged with palm trees—everything he hated, when you got down to it, including the Pernod-soaked card games and the calvados-fueled belote. They'd ended up forming a comfortable environment where he moved without effort, trusting his reflexes.

That was what was so precious—because he'd grown lazy through and through. He no longer shaved more than twice a week. Sometimes he stayed in one place for hours on end, staring straight ahead, thinking about nothing.

He'd left La Rochelle, which he'd loved, without giving it a thought; only when the train lurched into motion and his relatives began waving handkerchiefs had he felt a pang. And yet he couldn't manage to tear himself away from Libreville. He was stuck there. Seeing the boat in the outer harbor hadn't even made him want to leave, though he'd been depressed for days.

Everything disgusted him—especially himself. But his disgust, his listlessness, was something he needed. That was why he got so irritated when Adèle prolonged her steady gaze. She knew—and what she didn't know, she guessed.

Then how come she loved him, or was pretending to?

"I'm going to bed," he said, getting up.

He looked at the guests. They were all drunk. Today he didn't need to wait until closing time. Adèle was no longer the boss. It was Bouilloux who would shut down the generator, lock the doors and shutters, and go upstairs last, a candle in his hand.

"Good night, gentlemen."

Adèle rose when he did, and for the first time that night he felt satisfied. She'd made it seem entirely natural.

"Good-bye, friends!"

"Well, can't you give us a kiss? We're not going to see you again after you take off in the morning."

She made the rounds of the men gathered there, extending her cheek to each one. The one-eyed man was so excited he stroked her breast when he kissed her. She pretended not to notice.

"Coming?" she asked, walking up to Timar.

They went upstairs; the bursts of conversation went on behind them in the loud café. They were still in the same room, where Timar had slept on his first day in Africa.

"You were in some mood tonight. Not feeling well?"

"Me? I feel fine."

The same sequence of movements as on every other occasion: first she opened the mosquito net, then she smoothed down the sheet and plumped the pillows, after making sure the bed was free of scorpions or small snakes. At last she took off her dress the way she always did.

"We'll have to be up at five to get there before nightfall."

Timar took off his tie and looked at himself in the mirror. The mirror was dirty and the light from the candle weak. It was the puffiness around his eyes that made his reflection seem especially sinister.

He thought about Eugène, who'd been twice as strong as he was, and how he'd come down right in the middle of the party, his voice still not quite reduced to a croak, to say that snail fever was killing him.

He turned and saw Adèle naked. She was sitting on the edge of the bed, taking off her shoes.

"You're not getting undressed?"

At that precise moment, he thought, "Eugène is dead, but she's still here!"

He didn't draw any conclusions. It was better to leave things vague. He felt frightened and superstitious: he would go up there with her and, like Eugène, he would die; then, with someone else, maybe in this very room . . .

He took off his clothes and walked toward the bed.

"You're not going to put it out?"

He walked back to snuff out the candle.

"What time did you say?" he asked, making the bed frame creak.

"Five o'clock."

"Did you set the alarm?"

He turned his back to her, sought out the familiar hollow in the pillow, felt Adèle's hot flesh against his. She didn't say anything. He didn't, either. Not wanting to be the first to speak, he pretended to be asleep, but his eyes were open and his senses alert. He knew that she wasn't sleeping anymore than he was, that she was lying on her back, staring at the grayish glow of the ceiling.

It went on for a long time, so long that he almost fell asleep. He was just nodding off when he heard her voice say, "Night, Joe."

He didn't flinch, didn't move. It hadn't sounded exactly like Adèle's voice. Something had changed. Some three minutes passed before he felt the bed shake slightly, and suddenly he was awake again. He found himself sitting up, peering into the darkness.

"You're crying?"

She sobbed in response, as if he'd finally permitted her to show her feelings.

"Go to sleep," she said through her tears. "Go on!"

She forced him to lie back down. She wrapped an arm around his chest and wept with tenderness as she said, "Why are you so mean?"

7

THE FLATBOAT left the pier at first light. Bouilloux had brought Timar, Adèle, and their luggage in his little truck. The truck remained on the pier in the morning dusk, and Bouilloux waved as the vessel heaved over the first swell, righted itself, and disappeared again.

There it was—the ocean. To reach the mouth of the river, they had to cut through the waves. A black with an old sun helmet on his head was at the helm. He wore a cloth vest over black cotton bathing trunks, and it was hard to say why he didn't look ridiculous. He stared straight ahead, his face cryptic. His hands, which were paler than his body as a whole, held the steering wheel.

Adèle remained on her feet for as long as Bouilloux and his truck were visible, then went to sit in the stern. She was dressed just as she was every day, except that she had put on rubber boots to protect her legs against the mosquitoes.

This hour was the hardest to get through. They'd woken up too early, in the dark, and nervously packed their bags. Now the swell rocked them. It wasn't full daylight yet.

They didn't speak or look at each other. In spite of last night's scene, or maybe because of it, they seemed strangers. It was still painful to Timar. He couldn't have described what had happened, since he'd completely lost his self-control along with any sense of reality. That had been good.

"Why are you crying? Tell me why you're crying!"

As soon as he'd put the question to her, there'd been a shift. He'd been short with her, almost threatening, because he was sleepy and thought it was going to go on for a long time.

"Go to sleep! It's over!"

He had lit the candle, grown angry, accused Adèle of not understanding anything. He was the one who had a right to feel sad, not her! In the end he'd had a genuine fit, and, leaning over him, she had calmed him down. All this in the hot sheets, damp with tears and sweat. The end had been even more ridiculous: he had begged her to forgive him.

"No, Joe, sleep! You're going to toss and turn all night."

Hurt, he fell asleep with his head on her breasts. In the morning everything was forgotten; there was nothing between them, not a trace of feeling, just a coldness.

Half a mile out, they were running parallel to the line of palms. Once they were past the mouth of the harbor, they saw the coastline. A few minutes later, they entered the river just as the sun was coming up.

It was the end of the night—of everything ridiculous and awkward that had come with it. Timar turned to Adèle with laughing eyes, his vision caressing the scenery.

"Not too shabby."

"It's pretty."

He lit a cigarette, and at that moment he was full of optimism. Adèle was smiling, too. She got up to come closer and to look at the landscape with him, while the black handled the wheel and stared without expression at the horizon.

A few native boats stood immobile in the current. As they passed, they could make out some blacks, as motionless as their boats, who were fishing. The calm was unreal. It lifted the spirits. You wanted to sing something slow and powerful like a hymn to drown out the noise of the sawmill and the droning of the flatboat.

———

Gradually they gnawed away at the distance, leaving long stripes on the water behind. You could hear the propeller striking the water. They passed one tree, then another.

After the first bend, they left the sea behind and the sawmill that had been on the left, and there were just the two riverbanks and the vegetation growing as close as a yard away, which they sometimes even brushed against. The jungle was filled with picturesque trees, mangroves whose roots rose out of the ground and reached the height of a man, pale kapok trees with triangular trunks that didn't bear leaves except at the very top. Everywhere there were lianas and reeds, and silence, too, that the unrelenting drone of the motor sliced through like a plow.

"Is it very deep?" Timar asked naïvely, like someone taking a Sunday walk along the Marne.

The black didn't think the question was addressed to him. Adèle answered. "Here it's about a hundred feet. Other places we'll be scraping the bottom."

"Are there crocodiles?"

"You see them sometimes."

There was just one word for this moment: "vacation." Timar was on vacation—even the sun seemed happier than usual.

They saw the first black village: four or five huts set among the trees by the water where half a dozen native canoes were moored. Naked children watched the flatboat go by. A woman who was bathing sank down to her neck in the water and shouted.

"Are you hungry, Joe?"

"Not yet."

He felt like a tourist. He examined the landscape closely, missing nothing.

"Show me an okume tree."

She looked around. Finally she pointed out a tree.

"That's it? And it's worth a lot?"

"It's the only kind you can make plywood from. It's planed by machine. All the work's automated."

"How about a mahogany?"

"There aren't any around here. We'll start seeing them in an hour or two."

"And ebony?"

"Later on, too. Downstream all the valuable trees were cut down long ago."

"But where we'll be, there's still ebony?"

It was the first time he'd said "we."

"Ebony and mahogany, yes. Old Truffaut also gave me a pretty good idea. The concession is full of orchids. He gave me a book about them. Some of them sell for as much as fifty thousand francs each in Europe. And he found some that look just like the ones in the book."

Why was it all so beautiful that morning? Everything was working out. The landscape was full of promise. Was it even as hot as it had been on other days? Timar didn't take any notice.

They had been on the water for two hours when the flatboat veered toward the right bank, its bow coming to rest on a sandbank. The black, impassive as ever, threw a line to a woman standing there; she was naked except for a bunch of dried grass that covered her sex. Timar had never seen breasts like hers—large, heavy, and sumptuously full.

"What's going on?" he asked.

The black turned to him.

"Cool down engine."

There was a handful of native canoes, a village of maybe fifteen huts. Timar and Adèle leaped onto the bank while the black woman was laughing with the mechanic.

They were holding a market in the middle of a clearing. Five women, four of them very old, were squatting in front of the mats with some goods on display. Here, too, there was an absolute calm, while the natural hierarchy of things and beings, along with their natural proportions, seemed to have been reversed.

The trees were a hundred and fifty feet tall; at their feet, in middle of this limitless wilderness, a few handfuls of cassava, a couple of bananas, and five or six little smoked fish were displayed on mats. Two of the women were smoking a pipe. A third was breast-feeding a baby of about two, who from time to time turned to look curiously at the whites.

No contact between them and the natives, not even a greeting. Adèle went first, glancing at the little piles of merchandise and craning her neck to see into the huts. She leaned down and took a banana; she didn't bother to pay.

No hostility, either. They were whites, and they did whatever they wanted to—because they were whites.

Suddenly Adèle said, "Wait here for a second."

She strode toward the largest of the huts, which was off to one side. She went in without hesitation, while Timar stayed behind, looking at what passed for a market.

Did she know someone here? What had gotten into her head?

Bored with looking at the old women and their miserable food-stuffs, he went back to the flatboat. The black had gone ashore. He stood silhouetted in the light shining through the leaves and vines. Beside him was the naked young woman. They were standing right next to each other, but only their fingertips touched. They were laughing. Deep, slow syllables rose out of them, expressing nothing, it seemed, but satisfaction.

Timar didn't want to disturb them, so he turned and retraced his steps. Adèle wasn't back yet. He was about to go join her in the hut, but he didn't dare. With nothing to do, he took a pack of cigarettes from his pocket. A naked little boy made a begging face and stretched out his palm.

Three yards away, one of the old women stretched out her palm; he tossed her a cigarette and there was a mad scramble. All the black women crowded around, arms extended, bumping one another and quarreling over the tobacco. They shouted, laughed, pushed, and shoved, and dropped to their knees to look for the cigarette that had fallen on the ground. Adèle came up and smiled at the sight of Timar struggling with them.

"Let's go!" she said.

She took a second banana as she passed. It was only on board, when the engine had started back up, that he asked her where she'd gone.

"Don't worry about it."

"You know somebody in the village?"

"It doesn't matter."

The flatboat was making its way through air that had grown hotter and more humid. Timar felt a sudden unpleasant tightening in his chest.

"You're not going to tell me the truth?"

Her smile was sweet, submissive.

"I swear, it's nothing."

Something he thought he'd forgotten came back to him—one of his first experiences with women. Why was that? He'd been seventeen. He'd spent three days in Paris, and one night he'd allowed a woman to take him to a hotel in the rue Lepic. When they were downstairs again, in the hall, the woman had said, just like Adèle, "Wait here for a second."

She'd gone into the manager's office. He heard them murmuring, and when she'd come out again she was cheerful.

"Let's go."

"What were you doing in there?"

"Don't worry about it. Women's business."

It took him nearly three years to realize she'd gone in to collect her percentage of the price of the room.

What had made him think of that, here on the river? He couldn't say. Looking at Adèle, who was more animated than usual, he saw the other woman. He'd never learned her name.

"It was a black's place?"

"Of course! There aren't any whites here."

And because he was frowning, "Don't be that way, Joe. I swear—it's nothing."

Impassive as ever under his ragged, oily sun helmet, the black looked straight ahead. Every now and then, he gave a slight turn to the wheel.

———

Was the problem the incident at the hut? Exhaustion and the heat must have had done something to Timar's state of mind. The sun shone down overhead and the flatboat moved too slowly to make a cooling breeze. The unchanging landscape became oppressive.

He'd eaten a can of warm pâté and some stale bread. Already he'd had two shots of liquor.

It was his time for it. Around the middle of the afternoon, he'd get a hollow feeling in his chest. He only felt like himself after he'd had a touch of liquor.

Adèle was still in a good mood. Too good a mood—it seemed unnatural to Timar. Most of the time she didn't work so hard to make him happy. She was more direct than that—and more reserved.

What could she have been doing in the black man's hut? Why the smiles and playfulness now?

Finally, Timar sat down on the bottom of the boat, letting his gaze slip over the irregular treetops at the speed of the boat. His chest started to hurt again. "Hand me the bottle."

"Joe!"

"What? I don't have a right to be thirsty?"

She looked resigned as she handed him the flask of whiskey. He almost didn't hear her murmur, "Watch out."

"For what? Black women I can go visit in their huts?"

He knew he wasn't being fair. It had been happening a lot recently. He couldn't help himself.

At those moments, he was convinced that he was unhappy, that he was the one making all the sacrifices. It gave him the right to hate the whole world.

"You shouldn't gripe—you made a living getting people soused."

A rifle lay in the bottom of the boat in case they spotted some game, but they hadn't seen anything except for a few birds. The air was teeming with flies, though. One hand was always busy waving them out of your face. Timar knew the river was infested with tsetses; every time an insect landed on him, he jumped.

He stood up suddenly, at the end of his tether. He took off his jacket. Under it was just a short-sleeved shirt.

"That's a mistake, Joe. You'll get sick."

"So?"

It wasn't any cooler with his jacket off. On the contrary. But at least he didn't have that sticky sweaty feeling in his armpits and on his chest. It was a different sensation now—a feeling, almost voluptuous, of his flesh roasting through.

"Give me the bottle."

"You've had enough to drink."

"Give me the bottle, I said!"

And he insisted because he knew that the black, who seemed so impassive, was listening to everything and judging them both. He drank with greedy defiance, then lay down on the bench with his jacket rolled up under his head.

"Listen, Joe, the sun is strong and ..."

He didn't even bother to answer. He was sleepy. He was crushed with exhaustion. He was ready to drop dead, if it came to that. He couldn't have gotten up if he'd wanted to.

For several hours, he sank into a strange stupor. He slept, open-mouthed, and his body became a world of mysterious occurrences.

Was he a tree? A mountain? Two or three times, his eyelids parted and he saw Adèle trying to keep him in the shade.

Suddenly there was a catastrophic noise, a brutal, wrenching sensation that threw him under the bench. He picked himself up, haggard, with clenched fists and bulging eyes.

"What the hell is going on?"

The flatboat was leaning at an angle and the water was rushing madly past the gunwale. In a sort of semiconsciousness, Timar saw the black step over the rail. He thought he was coming to get him, that he'd been lured into an ambush, and he threw himself at the black man, knocking him into the water with a punch in the face.

"So that's what you want! We'll see about that!"

The water was no more than a foot and a half deep. The flatboat had drifted into some rapids. Painfully, the black climbed back into the boat. Timar was looking everywhere for the rifle he'd seen that morning.

"You bastard! You'll see..."

But he tripped over something, he wasn't sure what—the bench, maybe, or the gun he'd wanted. He stumbled. He fell and in a flash saw Adèle looking at him in horror, certainly in despair. His head struck something hard.

"Bastard!" he repeated.

And everything was spinning, everything moved, things flew up in the sky and the shadows came down from above.

Yet there were still moments of vague consciousness. One time, when he opened his eyes, he was sitting on the bottom of the boat; the black was holding him up while Adèle, struggling to lift his arms, was putting his jacket back on.

Another time, it was Adèle's face bent over him. He was lying down. His temples were a little cool and damp, while his hands, neck, and chest were roasting.

At last he was being carried. It wasn't just two people, but ten, a hundred! A multitude of blacks, their legs all moving at the height of his head.

They spoke a language he didn't recognize. Adèle was speaking it, too.

Through the black legs he could see trees, many trees, then a darkness from which a damp smell of compost rose.

8

HE WAS sitting on his bed, and what he noticed before anything else wasn't Adèle, who'd helped him up, but the walls. They were pale green. So he hadn't been dreaming. If one detail was real, everything was.

Timar frowned suspiciously. His mouth was set like a judge's.

"How long have I been here?"

He stared hard at Adèle, as if he wanted to catch her in a lie.

"Four days. Why are you looking at me that way?"

She was still putting him on. She laughed nervously, without meaning to.

"Give me a mirror!"

She went looking for it, and he ran his hand over his unshaved cheeks. He was thinner. He didn't recognize his eyes. And here he'd only made a few small gestures and was already tired.

"Where's Bouilloux?"

He knew he was upsetting her and the fact gave him pleasure. He guessed his feverish stare seemed threatening.

"Bouilloux? We're not in Libreville anymore. We're at home, at the concession."

"Where's Bouilloux?"

He had lots and lots of other questions, too. Questions? More like a case to prosecute. Because while he he'd been lying there with a fever of a hundred and five, he'd seen a lot and he'd heard a lot, too. And just as soon as he'd discovered that the room was green...

It was on the second day—in any case near the beginning— that Adèle, after settling them in, had looked at the walls with disgust. He heard her moving around downstairs, giving orders. Later on, she'd painted the partitions lime green.

She had no idea he'd seen her. His eyes had been wide open. She'd called someone else in to do the ceiling.

"What about Bouilloux?"

He wanted to get that question out of the way, because he had another waiting.

"He hasn't been here, Joe, I swear!"

So what? He'd see about Bouilloux later; he was almost positive he'd heard his voice from the first floor, that he'd even heard him say, "My poor little Adèle!"

Hadn't she opened the door a crack, at night, to let Bouilloux have a look at him?

"And the Greek?"

She couldn't lie because he was sure he'd seen that one, really seen him, and not once or twice but four or five times. A big fellow with greasy hair, a thin tanned face, and a tic: every few seconds he'd wink with his right eye.

"Constantinesco?"

Yes! After the walls were painted, she'd called for him to hold the ladder while she did the high bits. He had seen him clearly.

"What's he doing here?"

"He's the overseer. He's worked on the concession before, so I hired him. You've got to rest, Joe. You're soaked in sweat."

He needed to speak, to question her, to be cruel. There were certain things that he remembered with horror.

For instance, he'd been colder than he could ever have imagined in his life. And yet he was drenched in sweat, his teeth were chattering, and he'd cried out, "For God's sake, bring me some blankets! Somebody light a fire!"

Adèle had replied gently, "You already have four blankets."

"That's not true! I'm freezing to death! Where's the doctor? How come the doctor hasn't been called?"

He'd had hallucinations and nightmares. In the next bed, Timar saw Eugène looking at him with his dull stare.

"You're not used to it yet, kid. But you'll get there. I've already gone through it, you see."

Gone through it? How? Timar got angry, screamed, called out for Adèle. She was beside him.

If only he could have killed her! But he didn't have a gun. She was making fun of him. With Constantinesco, who came in on tiptoe, whispering, "Still a hundred and five?"

Now he'd get to the bottom of it all! He didn't have a fever anymore. He could see things clearly. He blinked to make sure he was seeing straight.

"I had snail fever, didn't I?"

"No, Joe. It wasn't snail fever at all. You had a bout of dengue fever, like everyone when they first get to the colonies. It isn't serious."

So it wasn't even serious!

"You must have been bitten by a fly on the river, and the sun helped to give you a violent fever. It shoots straight up to a hundred and five, but no one's ever died of it."

He tried to see if she'd changed. Was she wearing her boots? He leaned over to look. There they were on her feet.

"Why are you wearing those?"

"I have to go supervise the work site sometimes."

"What work site?"

"We're fixing the machines."

"Who?"

And that "who" was a threat.

"Constantinesco. He's a mechanic."

"Who else?"

"We have two hundred native workers who are busy building huts for themselves."

"We? Who's 'we'?"

"The two of us, Joe. You and me."

"Oh. Good."

He'd thought she meant her and Constantinesco. Timar was already worn out. The sweat on his body turned cold. Adèle was holding one of his hands and looking at him without sadness, with a hint of irony even, the way you look at a naughty child.

"Listen, Joe, you've got to try and rest. Tomorrow you can get up. Dengue fever knocks you down like that, but it goes away just as quickly. Tomorrow we'll have a nice long talk about the business. Everything's going well."

"Lie down beside me."

For a second she hesitated, for less than a second. He was ashamed because he knew that his bed reeked of sickness.

"Closer."

His eyes were half closed. He saw her through his eyelashes—a blur. He slid his hand down her legs.

"Don't tire yourself out, Joe."

Too bad! He needed to make sure she was his and he did, damp, trembling, with a surly look on his face. When he fell back onto his pillow, exhausted, his whole body coursing with anxiety, she got up calmly and adjusted her dress. Without any anger, she said, "You silly creature. You're just a boy, a great big boy..."

He could no longer hear her. All he could hear was his beating heart, the blood pulsing through his temples.

The following day, Adèle and Constantinesco helped him move down to the big room on the first floor. The Greek was slender, his hair was still black, and from a distance he looked young. Close up, however, his face turned out to be covered with wrinkles, its features irregular and unattractive. He was respectful, even fawning. When he spoke, he seemed to be fishing for Timar's approval.

The house was empty. They'd had to throw out practically everything they'd found there, the furniture and the other things, too, making a junk pile outside that they'd set on fire. They'd only kept a few things that were indispensable, tables, chairs, two beds. Even these had had to be disinfected.

They put Timar in a kind of sofa-cum-hammock. His room was enormous. It opened onto the veranda on three sides, and the red-brick walls inside gave it a very colonial look. Outside, the land descended steeply to the river, where a hundred and fifty blacks were busy building huts. On the other three sides of the house, less than five hundred yards away, there was jungle.

"Where does Constantinesco sleep?" he asked with a trace of feeling.

"In a hut like the natives. It's out behind the shed."

"Who does he eat with?"

"He keeps a black woman. They live together."

He had a hard time suppressing a smile; he turned his head because he was sure Adèle had noticed.

"You see, Joe, it's just like I told you: the house is solid and practical, and the concession—I've been all around it—is the best in Gabon. I've already found workers. Now you rest for a couple of days. Constantinesco can handle the work."

"Yes."

Still, he was depressed. He knew he'd need more than a couple of days of rest to work like the others. He saw them coming and going under the sun, while just the thought of going out onto the veranda, with its reflected glare, made him physically ill.

What good was he, then? Adèle was so relaxed, so straightforward in her black silk dress, with her white sun helmet and rubber boots. She strolled freely among the blacks, speaking their dialect and giving orders as if she'd been doing it all her life. She'd found a few mildewed books among the things old Truffaut left behind: a Maupassant, a Loti, and a chemistry textbook.

He wasn't up to reading the novels. In Europe, he'd have devoured them. Here, he had to wonder why people bothered to print so many words.

When Adèle rejoined him, she found him deep in the chemistry book.

———

The days passed. To Timar they all seemed alike. In the morning he came downstairs, alone or leaning on Adèle's arm. He settled down in the big room. Every once in a while he got up and took a couple of steps.

All around him people were already at work. Constantinesco had sounded the bell at six. He showed up in boots, horsewhip in hand, to make his report to Adèle. She didn't ask him to sit down and treated him like a stranger.

"I left twenty men to finish the huts. I sent the rest of them into the woods. The tables for the house will be finished tonight. And I sent the hunter out for a buffalo to feed the blacks."

Timar was amazed at all the work that had been done while he was sick. And yet, to the best of his recollection, each time he opened his eyes Adèle had been sitting at the head of his bed. That hadn't prevented her from organizing and directing everything. It was true that she looked paler, that the circles under her eyes were darker.

"We should build a shed for the flatboat; if we don't, the motor won't work when we need it."

"I thought of that. Two men are digging postholes to the left of the workers' camp."

Now Adèle and Timar were alone. She went on talking.

"You'll see, Joe, you'll get used to it. This is one of the healthiest parts of the country. In three years, we'll return to France with our million."

That was exactly what horrified Timar. He didn't want to go back to France. To do what? Where would he settle down? Would he go back to his family? Would he leave Adèle?

The two novels he'd tried to read had made it clear to him that there was no longer a place for him anywhere. He'd never be able to go back to La Rochelle and spend hours with his friends on the terrace of the Café de la Paix.

Live in Paris with Adèle? But Adèle, in France...

No—best not to think about it. He'd see. Meanwhile, he tried to acclimatize himself, to develop regular habits, to familiarize himself with the land. In a few days he'd be able to go out. He would oversee the blacks he saw milling around down by the water. He'd go into the jungle and pick out the trees for cutting.

He still felt all too drained. Just walking for ten minutes around the room—the floor was red brick like the walls—made him so dizzy that he had to sit down.

"Are you sure Bouilloux wasn't here when I was sick?"

"Why do you ask?" She laughed—the same laugh as when he'd asked her about her visit to the black man's hut. So much the same, that he was left suspended between relief and suspicion, hatred and love.

When she wasn't around he worried. He'd drag himself out to the veranda a hundred times to see if she was back. What really calmed him was when he spotted Constantinesco off in the distance in a direction opposite from the one in which she'd gone.

On the third day he felt genuine joy. Ignoring Adèle's advice, he left the house. Sixty blacks, lashed to an enormous log of okume wood, were dragging it on rollers to the river.

The first tree! His first tree! His legs shaky, he prowled around the almost-naked black workers, smelling their pungent odor. Constantinesco, in his boots as always, hurled orders in dialect from behind. The log inched forward. Bodies glistened with sweat. The workers panted.

"How much is that worth?" Timar asked Adèle when she came back.

"About eight hundred francs a ton, but shipping's three hundred a ton. That log represents a profit of two thousand francs."

He was surprised that such a huge block of wood wasn't worth more.

"What if it was mahogany?"

She didn't answer; she was listening to something.

He heard it, too: the distant drone of an engine.

"A flatboat!"

The log was still descending toward the riverbank and some men had waded into the water to haul it down. It was evening; in half an hour it would be night. Constantinesco, who'd been in Gabon for twenty years, had long since taken off his sun helmet.

The log, solidly tethered like a huge captured beast, began to float. Just then a flatboat rounded the bend and ran up onto the sand.

The boat contained two blacks and a white man, who jumped on shore and shook Adèle's hand.

"All settled in?"

It was the provisions. Each month the same flatboat came up-river to serve all the little outposts, bringing mail and necessities to the loggers.

"You must be thirsty. Come on up to the house."

The young man drank a whiskey first, then pulled a letter for Timar out of his bag. It bore a French stamp. The handwriting was his sister's. After reading a few lines he shoved it into his pocket.

My dear Joe,

I'm writing to you from Royan, where we've come for the day. The weather is nice, but I'm sure less nice than in the wonderful land where you have the good fortune to live. The Germain boys are here with us, and soon we'll all be setting off to go aquaplaning . . .

"Anything for me?" asked Adèle.

"No. Oh—yes. Can you imagine? Bouilloux's engine gave out as he was headed back downriver. He had to spend the night in a village."

Timar turned quickly to Adèle. She was unfazed and didn't blush.

"Oh," she said noncommittally.

But now her gaiety seemed forced.

"What are they saying down there?"

"Not much."

They were in the big red-brick room, where there were only three deck chairs and a table. Down by the river, the black workers who had dragged the okume log were laughing and sponging themselves off. Constantinesco was walking over to the bell with which he signaled the beginning and the end of the workday.

"As to the Thomas business . . ."

The young man paused before speaking. He seemed a decent fellow, a little awkward and shy. He spent three weeks a month in the flatboat with two blacks, going upriver and then coming back down, spending his nights under a tent in the jungle. In France he'd been a traveling salesman specializing in remote villages, where he sold complete trousseaux on the installment plan. In Gabon, he practiced his trade with the same awkwardness, the same bluff humor that he'd displayed in the hamlets of Normandy and Brittany.

"They caught the murderer. A black guy, naturally."

Adèle didn't move a muscle. She was quite calm. She glanced from Timar to the traveler.

"He was arrested two days after you left. I mean the chief of his village turned him in. Since then it's been nothing but talk, talk, talk, day in and day out. The chief brought witnesses."

Timar, leaning toward the young man, was breathing hard.

"And then?"

"The black played dumb. He swore he didn't know anything about it. Since everything has to be translated in these cases, things don't move quickly—even after they found the pistol buried in his hut. The witnesses do say that the accused was after the same woman as Thomas.

"By the way, what can I offer you? I have some excellent canned lobster. If you need gas, I have twenty cans."

Timar was no longer listening. He looked at Adèle, who said, "Get the twenty cans. And two sacks of rice for our workers. Do you have any cigarettes? I can sell them for three francs a pack."

"I'll give you a thousand for a zinc franc."

Night fell. You could hardly see the river. Constantinesco started the electric generator, and the lights glowed red, then yellow.

"With five or six zincs . . ."

"Tell me! The man they arrested, what village was he from?"

"Joe! Enough!"

"I've got a right to—"

"A little village downstream."

Timar got up and went to sit on the veranda. He could just make out the silhouette of the log floating like a ship at anchor. The blacks had lit a fire in the middle of their circle of huts. Around the house the jungle was black as ink, except for the white trunk of a kapok tree soaring straight up to the sky.

He was sure that he heard or, with his heightened senses, positively divined the words that Adèle whispered between clenched teeth to the salesman: "You idiot!"

9

"BE QUIET, Joe, I'm begging you—he can hear!"

The voice was a just whisper, and Timar could barely make out her face, still, staring up at the ceiling. The room was pitch-black. The only light came from the rectangular open window. The white trunk of the kapok tree divided it into two unequal sections.

They were naked on the bed. A few moments earlier, they could still hear the salesman moving around in the next room.

"Tell the truth!"

Timar spoke sharply, without moving. He was looking into emptiness, or rather the darkness overhead. As to Adèle, all he could feel was her elbow and thigh.

"Wait till tomorrow. I'll tell you when we're alone."

"Tell me now!"

"What do you want me to say?"

"You killed Thomas!"

"Hush!"

She didn't move. Her thigh didn't stir. They lay without moving, side by side.

"So? Come on, tell me—you killed him, didn't you?"

He waited, holding his breath. Her voice was calm in the darkness. "Yes."

Suddenly he turned, grabbing a wrist at random. He groaned. "You killed him and you pinned the blame on someone else! Tell me! You killed him and then you went into that hut and you—"

"I'm begging you, Joe! You're hurting me!"

It was a cry of real physical pain. Timar was hunched over her. He was squeezing hard.

"Listen! I swear I'll tell you everything tomorrow."

"What if I don't want an explanation? What if I don't want to see you anymore or hear anything more from you again? What if..."

He choked on his words. He was sweating more than ever, and he felt weak in all his extremities. He was so angry that he had to do something, he didn't know what—kill her or put his fist through the wall. Adèle was trying to stop him. No use.

"Joe...listen. He can hear us...I'll tell you, just be quiet!"

Fists bruised, he stopped hitting her. He looked at her blindly. Was there some other way to control his anger?

They were standing, their bodies like two pale smudges in the room. They had to strain to see each other, and yet Adèle was wiping Timar's chest with his damp handkerchief.

"Go to bed! You'll have another attack!"

True. He could feel it. He remembered how sick he'd been and quieted down right away. He found a chair in the darkness, pulled it toward him, and sat.

"Go on! I'm listening."

He didn't want her to be near lest he hurt her again. He was trying to keep calm, but he was trying too hard. It seemed unhealthy.

"You just want me to tell you, like that?"

She didn't know what to do with herself. She ended up sitting at the end of Timar's bed.

"You didn't know Eugène. He was jealous, especially toward the end, when he knew he was going to die."

She spoke in a whisper so as not to be heard in the next room.

"Jealous? He seemed to get on fine with Bouilloux, the governor, the prosecutor, and everyone else who slept with you."

He couldn't see her, but from the interruption in her breathing he could tell she was swallowing hard. At one point it was so quiet that you could hear the jungle outside the window—its immense living silence.

Adèle blew her nose. She said steadily, "You don't understand. It's not the same thing. I came to you as..."

She couldn't find the word. Perhaps the word that had come to her lips sounded too romantic? As a lover?

"It's not the same," she said again. "Listen! Thomas saw me come out. He wanted a thousand francs. He'd wanted the money for a long time—to buy a woman. I told him no. And when he brought it up again on the night of the party—"

"You killed him." Timar's voice uttered dreamily from the shadows.

"He was going to talk!"

"If it was because of me . . ."

Her response was quiet and frank. "No! I killed him so he'd leave me in peace. I couldn't have known that Eugène was going to die anyway."

And Timar tried to hold on to the shaky self-control that was keeping him from going mad. He stared at the rectangle of the window and the trunk of the kapok tree. He listened to the jungle rustling.

"Come to bed, Joe."

It was too much. Once again, he felt like screaming, like punching the wall. She'd owned up to everything and she wanted him to lie down beside her, right next to her warm naked body.

It was too simple—she'd committed murder to be left in peace. And he, with his questions, was keeping her from enjoying the repose she so richly deserved. She hadn't denied it when he'd mentioned the governor and the others. But that wasn't the same thing. He couldn't understand—unlike her husband, who had!

There were moments when he wondered if he'd get up and hit her, hit her until he was completely worn out.

"And the black they arrested?"

"Would you be happier if I went to jail for ten years?"

"Stop it! No! Don't say another word, leave me alone!"

"Joe!"

"I'm begging you, shut up!"

He stood and leaned on the window frame. The night air froze the sweat running down his skin. He saw a reflection on the surface of the river, close to the tethered log. He'd been standing there for something like five minutes when a voice behind him said, "Aren't you coming to bed?"

He didn't answer—or move. But he wasn't only thinking about Adèle—and certainly not about Thomas. His thoughts wandered. He said to himself, for instance, that not far away there were leopards, that at about this time in Europe everyone would be leaving the beachfront casinos.

Maybe, in some of those casinos, they'd shown exotic films, with banana trees, a plantation owner with a fine mustache, and a love scene accompanied by native music.

His thoughts reverted to the log. In the rainy season it would flow downstream with the current along with all the other trees that had been cut. Hundreds of logs would be hoisted aboard a little red-and-black steamboat anchored fore and aft in the estuary. First they would float past the little village where Adèle had gone into the hut.

How they'd laughed, laughed until all their teeth showed, and never said a thing—the black boat pilot and the pretty girl with the naked breasts by the river.

So Eugène, when he was still alive, hadn't minded his wife taking lovers—as long as they were influential men who'd help them make their fortune. Wasn't that how the two of them had operated, in any case?

He turned. He saw Adèle's open eyes and pretended to slip back into a trance. He was sleepy. He was a little cold. To put a good face on things, he lit a cigarette.

What was he going to do? The concession was in his name. He'd staked the credit of his uncle and his family.

Out in the jungle there must be elephants. Constantinesco had told him so that afternoon.

Was Adèle sleeping with Constantinesco, too? He could hear her breathing more loudly and more steadily. He took advantage of that to slip into the bed.

Maybe he'd been wrong—because he kept thinking that

afterward her breathing had changed. She was pretending to be asleep, or maybe he'd woken her up and now she was controlling her breathing.

They weren't touching and they couldn't see each other, but each of them knew the other was there. The slightest tremor was multiplied a thousand times.

She didn't get it! At the end of the day, she acted by impulse and the way she'd been brought up to. Still, it hadn't seemed like she'd sleep with just anyone. All those kisses hadn't left a scar—or any trace at all! He liked her indolence and her yielding flesh. He was amazed by her directness.

What did the elephants do out there in the night? Wander around like other smaller animals? Timar must have been half asleep, since he could hear himself breathing like someone who was asleep. Adèle reached out and touched him on the chest at the level of his heart.

He didn't move, he didn't let her guess that he wasn't in fact fast asleep. He remembered nothing after that apart from the noise of the clock and the bands of light and shadow.

He opened his eyes. It was day. He heard the workers heading out into the jungle. Timar's hand groped the other side of the bed. No Adèle. The sheets were already cold.

He stayed in bed another fifteen minutes; he looked at the ceiling and was astonished to find himself so tranquil. He was like a convalescent who'd exhausted all his strength at one go. His fists hurt. He'd split the skin on his knuckles.

Finally he got up, slipped into his pants and shirt, and pushed his hair out of his face. Downstairs he found the traveling salesman eating breakfast and reading an old newspaper.

"Sleep well?"

Timar looked for Adèle. All he could see was Constantinesco in the courtyard, giving orders to some half-dozen blacks.

"Did she go out?"

There was nothing to say, but he missed her. He needed to see her, if only to ignore her.

"She left you a message."

Timar found himself in front of a mirror. He looked at himself. His face was expressionless. It amazed him. He felt proud. And yet within everything was utter turmoil.

"A message?"

The salesman handed him a piece of paper. Timar realized he'd never seen Adèle's handwriting. The letters were careful and too big.

My Joe,

Don't be upset. I had to go to Libreville, but I'll be back in two or three days at the latest. Take care of yourself. Constantinesco knows what to do. Above all, try to stay calm, please.

Your Adèle

"So she caught the first train?" Timar said in a biting tone.

"She must have taken the flatboat in the night, because when I got up an hour ago she was already gone."

There was nothing for Timar to add. He paced the room, face set, hands behind his back.

"You know, it's nothing serious. I was the one who brought the news. The prosecutor needs to see her to wind up this business with the blacks."

"Oh—it was you who..."

And Timar shot him a look of contempt.

"It's all set. From the moment they had a suspect in hand it was all over. But for form's sake they have to speak to her, given it was her gun that—"

"Obviously."

"Where are you going?"

Timar went up to his room, shaved, and got dressed with unusually rapid, decisive motions. He went back downstairs and asked the salesman, "Could you rent me your flatboat?"

"That's impossible. I've just started on my rounds."

"Two thousand."

"I swear, I—"

"Five thousand!"

"Not even for fifty thousand! It's not my flatboat, it's the company's. If I didn't have the mail . . ."

Timar went outside without a look. The sound of an engine came from the machine shop, where Constantinesco was working. He was lying on the ground adjusting the generator.

"Did you know about it?" Timar asked without a hello.

"Well, I—"

"Fine! I want a canoe and men to paddle it. In five minutes."

"But—"

"Did you understand me?"

"When she left she said—"

"Who's boss here?"

"Listen, Mr. Timar, you're not going to like it, but no. I'm doing it for your own good. In your condition—"

"My condition what?"

"I have to refuse—absolutely."

Timar had never felt so calm—and he'd never had so many good reasons to blow his top. He felt capable of using his gun and shooting the Greek in cold blood, of heading off in a canoe even if there was no one else with him.

"I'm pleading with you—think it over. Later on—"

"Now!"

Already the sun was hot. Constantinesco put on his sun helmet, left the shop, and headed over to the huts by the water. The salesman's flatboat was still there and Timar thought of taking it without permission. But why make things messy?

The Greek spoke to several blacks who were standing around him. They looked at Timar, then at the canoes, then down the river.

"So?"

"They say it's late. They say they'll have to stop at night."

"That doesn't matter."

"They also say that it'll take three days to get back—because of the current."

The Greek looked at Timar more sorry than surprised. He must have seen similar cases. He was following the progress of the attack the way a doctor follows the course of a disease.

"Then I'm coming with you."

"Not on your life! You stay here—keep an eye on the concession. I don't want the work to stop at any cost."

Constantinesco issued a few more orders to the blacks, then followed Timar back to the house.

"Let me offer you some advice. First thing, don't let your men drink any alcohol, and don't drink any yourself. In a flatboat you get some air because of its speed—in a canoe the sun is a lot more dangerous. Take the folding cot in case you have to sleep in the brush. Then—"

He was more agitated than Timar.

"Let me come with you! You're scaring me! Think how your turning up is going to make a mess of everything! On her own, Madame Adèle is sure to succeed, but if—"

"She's told you things?"

Constantinesco frowned.

"No! But I've seen it all before. I know how things happen. You come from Europe. You see life differently. Once you've been in Gabon for ten years—"

"I'll probably get my kicks killing blacks."

"One of these days you're going to have to do it."

"You've had to do it, have you?"

"I came at a time when, in the jungle, whites were greeted with volleys of arrows."

"And you responded with bullets?"

"I knew a guy who only survived by throwing a stick of dynamite at them. Have you had something to eat? Believe me—eat first, think it over—"

"And don't go!" Timar shouted. "Thanks a lot... You're still here, you?"

It was the salesman, getting ready to leave. He said to Constantinesco, "Anything you want me to take farther on up?"

That meant upstream, where the jungle was thicker.

"Speaking of which, I'm going to see that fellow you were supposed to replace. You know—the one who promises he's going to shoot you."

A few minutes later, the three white men were standing by the water, near the okume log. Two blacks started up the salesman's flatboat. It made a semicircle and turned into the current.

Twelve natives were waiting by a canoe that had been loaded with bananas, palm oil, and cassava. The air was scorching. Every breath of wind was like a burning caress. Constantinesco looked Timar in the eyes as if to say, "It's still not too late."

Timar lit a cigarette and offered the pack to the Greek.

"Thanks, I don't smoke."

"Too bad for you."

Pointless words—he'd said them just to fill the emptiness. Timar looked uphill toward the house, the newly built native huts with their banana-leaf roofs, and, high up, a window facing a kapok tree. Last night he'd been looking out of that window into the jungle.

"Let's go!" he said suddenly.

The paddlers understood and climbed into the canoe, all but the chief, who waited to help the white man in.

Constantinesco hesitated before saying, "I'm sorry, but... you're not going to get her in trouble, are you? Please don't make matters any worse. She's an admirable woman."

Timar gave Constantinesco a hard look and almost said something. But no—what good would that do? He sat down, scowling, in the bottom of the canoe. Twelve carved paddles rose as one before plunging into the water.

The house disappeared quickly. There was little to see apart from the red-tile roof, then nothing—only the top of the kapok tree towering over the forest. The last time he'd looked at that milky trunk he'd been in bed beside Adèle, who'd been naked, within his reach, counting her breaths and pretending to sleep. And he'd refused to say a thing. Maybe a single word would have been enough, or touching her arm.

She'd touched him later, furtively. He'd acted like he hadn't noticed.

Now he felt like bursting into tears, out of disgust, desire, despair, just because he wanted her.

They were on the same river, maybe twenty miles apart. She was on the flatboat with the black; he lay crammed in the bottom of a rocking canoe. Twelve paddles rose out of the water together, dripping liquid pearls in the sunlight. They hung suspended for a moment and then came down, while the men lifted their voices in a sad unchanging chant whose muted powerful rhythm would be with them throughout the trip.

IO

A BLACK with rotting teeth yelled out a string of words. The instant all the paddles rose in the air, he fell silent—an interruption in the canoe's pulsing life.

Then twelve voices called back in response, chanting vigorously, and the paddles plunged into the water twice.

The little man started all over again in his high falsetto voice.

Two strokes of the paddle—that was the rhythm, exactly. Then the same brief pause, and the fury of the chorus calling back.

The whole exercise had been repeated something like five hundred times, and Timar—neck straining, his eyes narrowed—had started to anticipate the moment when the leader would once again drone out his bit. And he'd noticed that for the last hour it had always been exactly the same thing—maybe with the change of a word or two. The little fellow recited his piece without feeling, while various expressions—sometimes laughing, sometimes surprised, sometimes smiling—passed over his companions' faces as the couplets sounded.

And always, just when the twelve paddles hung suspended in the air, the twelve voices burst out energetically.

Suddenly, Timar was startled to realize what he was thinking about. He was amazed to find himself observing the blacks in a spirit of friendly curiosity, feeling quite calm and at peace. He felt thwarted, as if he'd been cheating someone—himself—in the drama he was playing out.

Even so, he went back to examining the natives one by one. Sometimes the river was rough, sometimes calm. Sometimes, notwithstanding the best efforts of the men, the canoe spun sideways. Each stroke of the paddle was followed by a great shock, a shudder that shook the canoe from stem to stern—at first it had made Timar uneasy. Now he was used to it, just as he was used to the smell of the blacks. Most of them wore loincloths, but three were completely naked.

The blacks faced forward, looking at the white man in front. They looked at him as they sang or when they laughed at a funny verse and as they plied their paddles with an air of fierce resolve.

Timar wondered if they were judging him, if they spared him any thought beyond generalities. It was the first time he'd looked at blacks as something other than objects of curiosity, picturesque, with their skins tattooed or actually carved up, some with silver rings in their ears, one with a clay pipe stuck in his frizzy hair.

Now he looked at them as human beings, trying to grasp their lives from that point of view, and it all seemed very simple to him, thanks perhaps to the jungle, the canoe, and the current carrying them along as for centuries it had carried identical canoes to the sea.

It seemed a lot simpler than, for example, the blacks in Libreville with their clothes, or boys like Thomas.

A photograph of the whole scene would have been picturesque: Timar thought of the little exclamations of his sisters and girl-friends, his friends' knowing smiles. A classic image of the colonial life, for sure: the canoe, Timar in front in his white outfit with a cork helmet on his head; without saying a word, the blacks had built him a canopy of banana leaves that made him look, if not re-gal, at least important; then, for the length of the canoe, the naked or half-naked paddlers standing one behind the other.

But it wasn't even picturesque—it was natural, soothing. It made Timar forget about himself—or anything at all. He took in images, sensations, smells, and sounds while the heat smothered him and the glare forced him to keep his eyes half shut.

Basically, the blacks seemed like good people, if a little back-ward, crying out in piercing voices when the canoe passed a village or even an isolated hut. Then they pushed the canoe to dizzying speeds. Brandishing their paddles over their heads, they all yelled together in joy and pride; other cries echoed from the bank in reply.

At one point, some black children dived into the water to try to race them. One of them was cheeky enough to say to Timar, "Cigarette! Give cigarette!"

The boy pretended to throw cigarettes into the river. Timar tossed a handful, and from afar saw the children fighting over them, soaking wet, in a great fireworks display of splashing, before they tore off into the bush.

———

An immense feeling of peace, that's what he was experiencing, but a peace tinged with sadness—he didn't know why. He had tenderness to spare within him, though it lacked a precise object, and it seemed to him that he was on the verge of understanding this land of Africa, which had provoked him so far to nothing but an unhealthy exaltation.

The river was calm, and the blacks steered the canoe to the bank and tied it up. Timar wasn't scared, he didn't feel the least twinge of apprehension, though he was the only one there who didn't speak the language. To the contrary—he felt as though they'd all taken him under their wing, like a child entrusted to their care.

They stood knee-deep and waist-deep in the water and washed their bodies. They took mouthfuls of water, gargled, and then spat.

Timar wanted to savor the sensation of the cool water, too. He got up, but the singer with the rotting teeth guessed what he was thinking. He shook his head, "Not good white man."

Not good for white people. How come? Timar didn't know, but he took it on faith. The man told him to eat, so he opened a can of pâté. The blacks contented themselves with cassava and bananas. The jungle was dark. At one point, the men were all ears, leaning forward and smiling. Timar looked at them inquisitively. One of them made a face and burst out laughing. "Macaque," he said.

They didn't see the monkey. They could only hear it in the branches. The sun was high up in the sky. Timar took some sips of whiskey—two or three. Soon he felt a luxurious sleepiness.

He was still examining the paddlers and without thinking playing a little game. It consisted of finding resemblances between them and people he knew in Europe.

His thoughts turned from France to Libreville, to the governor, the police chief, Bouilloux, and Adèle. The spell was thoroughly broken. He no longer looked around. He closed his eyes and felt the stirrings of a crisis.

It was like an angry swelling in his chest. He wanted to drink so as to do something bad, to scream, to make someone else suffer—himself, too. During one of these moments, he opened his eyes halfway and shouted to the blacks, who were chanting monotonously as always, "Silence! Shut up!"

They didn't understand right away. Then the man with the rotting teeth, who must have known a little French, turned to his companions and translated. There wasn't a word of protest. They simply fell silent, still looking at the white man: twelve pairs of eyes betraying no emotion at all. That upset Timar, especially since he wanted a drink. People like that—you shot them dead with a pistol!

Hadn't he been told that, the way they were, any one of them was capable of poisoning you in complete innocence?

The word "innocence" made him sneer. That was delicious! Here you could kill "in innocence"—that was it! Whites killed blacks and blacks killed each other, and sometimes, sometimes, they attacked a European. With no feeling. Because you have to live. No one was really a murderer. Maybe the little man with stumps for teeth had killed a few people. With tiny thorns steeped in poison—you put them in someone's food and let them slowly tear out their guts. Or with poisoned needles strewn at the entrance of your victim's hut.

They stopped again. Timar asked why. It was because the sun had shifted and was now falling on the nape of his neck. Two blacks brought banana leaves to shield him. Blacks who'd probably done their share of poisoning, too!

He drank more, but it didn't have the same effect as on other days. He didn't get angry or feel anxious. He lay back, eyes closed, unhappy and brooding.

Only when night fell did he return to reality. Darkness spread across the sky like an oil stain. There was no sunset to give relief. They were on a sluggish part of the river. It was wide, and the water was black around the canoe and especially along the bank under the trees. Somewhere far off a drum was beating, and the men, who'd been forbidden to sing by the white man, had to make do with a little grunt at every beat.

It was pointless to ask where they were. No one would understand, and in any case Timar wouldn't understand the answer. Where was he going to sleep? What was he doing here? Adèle had promised him she'd be back in two or three days. Why hadn't he waited for her at the house, where at least there was another white man?

What would he do in Libreville? He had absolutely no idea. When you got down to it, he hadn't wanted to be treated like a child, he'd been afraid of being taken for an accomplice, and he was jealous. Jealous above all. What had Bouilloux come to the concession for? Why had Adèle lied?

His worries returned. He drank a mouthful of warm liquor, and it soothed his stomach enough for him to lift his head and take a look around.

Night surrounded the canoe on all sides, and the men were no longer paddling in unison. They were going at it frantically. Sometimes two paddles struck together. And, instead of looking at the white man, their eyes strayed toward the jungle. Then, with a great heave, the canoe ran up onto the bank, lodging its prow in the undergrowth.

Only on land did Timar recognize where they were—in the village with the market where he'd stopped with Adèle on their way up-river, where she'd eaten two bananas and gone into the hut of a black.

There was a fire in the middle of a clearing surrounded by huts. Shadows squatted around it; Timar was afraid to go closer. He waited for the others, especially the man with the rotten teeth. Timar considered him to be his guardian.

The villagers didn't get up. They just turned their heads to observe the commotion down by the river. The folding cot and Timar's provisions were taken out of the canoe. Three paddlers carried everything to the center of the village. The puny fellow signaled for Timar to follow.

Not much was said—a few words at most. The man opened the doors to the huts, looked inside, and none of the occupants protested. From one of the huts he evicted the old woman who, only days before, had been squatting in front of her display at the market.

The cot and the provisions were placed in the hut. The black threw out the matting and, pointing at the décor, earnestly said, "Good! Here good!"

He went off after that without a noise, leaving Timar alone in the lighted hut. Only in the middle of it could he stand. It reeked of smoke: inside the fire must have been burning all day; the embers were still hot.

For ten minutes or so Timar struggled with the folding cot—he didn't know how to set it up. Finally he succeeded and made his way to the door, where he stood, smoking a cigarette. His paddlers had joined the villagers around the fire. He could only see their outlines, but they were all eating, using their hands to scoop boiled cassava from earthen plates.

Someone kept talking—loud and fluent like the singer in the canoe. Maybe it was him; the voice was the same. A few phrases came out very quickly, and they all sounded alike. Then he'd fall silent. Instead of the paddlers' refrain, there was a burst of laughter from the assembly.

Were they talking about Timar? For a moment he thought so, but a glance at the faces in the firelight convinced him that they weren't talking about anything. He could have sworn that the man with the bad teeth was just speaking nonsense, talking for talking's sake, that everyone was carried away by his meaningless words and by the sound of their own laughter. They were amusing themselves like children, talking up a storm without bothering over what it meant.

It smelled of burned wood, of spices Timar didn't recognize, and there was the blacks' own lingering smell. That was what was troubling him now.

He wasn't hungry. He didn't want to open a can of food. It was enough to take a sip of alcohol every now and then, followed by a cigarette. Everyone must have seen him, a white silhouette against the dark entrance to the hut, but no one was looking at him. Timar felt mortified by it, almost regretful.

"Cigarette?" he cried out, throwing one at the nearest black.

He'd found twenty packs in the folding cot. Constantinesco must have put them there. The black picked up the cigarette, rose, paused, then burst into laughter as he showed the others. An old woman turned around. She hesitated for a moment before stretching out her hands.

Timar tossed out a whole pack and the shadows dived for it, shoving one another, while the more enterprising ran right up to him, their hands outstretched, laughing and shouting, men and women together. Timar could smell them all around him, brushing against him. He was standing on tiptoe, reaching over their heads.

The smell from the moving mass of people grew stronger. There were young girls there, too, their small breasts barely formed. But the only one who caught Timar's attention was the pretty girl he'd seen by the river laughing with the mechanic from the flatboat the other day.

She was very near him, not so bold as the youngest ones. Her eyes were begging him to throw some cigarettes her way.

Timar threw her three, one after the other. Each time the cigarette was snapped up in flight or fell to the ground, where the children fought for it underfoot.

Her breasts were large and firm. Her thighs were an adolescent's, not so filled out as her chest, but her stomach was round like child's still. The two of them looked at each other through the excitement. She was pleading and he could only smile.

He threw the last pack of cigarettes in her direction. Timar shouted, "That's it! All gone!"

But they kept on stretching out their hands, until at last the puny fellow with the bad teeth explained that the white man had nothing more to give away. The group scattered as quickly as it had formed. A moment later, they were all squatting around the fire. Thick lips gripping their cigarettes, the blacks exhaled and watched the smoke with pride. Often three or four people smoked the same cigarette.

———

Timar was alone in front of his hut. He was about to go to bed, but he kept thinking about the black girl, not out of coarse desire but because he yearned for tenderness. He sat on a very low bench. He'd forgotten to save some cigarettes for himself. Women lugged babies into the huts, which fell silent. No more wood was thrown on the fire and the paddlers were the first to wander off.

Where were they going to sleep? Timar had no idea, and it didn't matter. He looked around for the girl, who had disappeared, and he wondered when she had left her companions and which hut she'd gone to. He went on feeling the same sad composure, a heavy animal sadness. There were only five or six shadowy figures left around the fire now. No one spoke. He looked to his left and right.

And suddenly he was trembling. The black girl was there,

standing in a shadow, leaning against the wall of the next hut and facing him. Had she sensed his desire? Did she feel something for him or was she just being submissive because he was white?

No doubt Bouilloux would have pointed his finger at the hut and followed her in. Timar didn't dare, and he was afraid to approach her. He felt awkward. In any case he hadn't decided to summon her.

He just stood there. And she came closer, step by step, ready to retreat if he didn't want her. He stood on the threshold of the hut, leaving enough space for her to go by. With a wave of his hand he showed her in.

She came inside quickly and stopped, her chest heaving. None of the blacks around the fire turned to look. He wasn't sure if he should close the door; he was afraid to. What would he say? She wouldn't understand a single word.

She was no longer looking at him. She was staring at the ground, like a young girl in Europe, just as self-conscious, the only difference being that she was naked apart from a tuft of grass.

He tapped her on the shoulder. It was the first time he'd touched a black of his own accord. The skin was smooth. He could feel the muscles stirring underneath.

He pretended to hunt for some cigarettes, though he knew he wouldn't find any. He wanted to give her something. In the folding cot there was nothing except for a thermos. He patted his pockets. His hand felt his watch, a present from his uncle. It was held by a chain, which he suddenly took off and handed to her.

"For you."

He was wracked with anxiety. Turning around, he noticed the blacks had left the fire. What was he going to do? What did he want to do? Did he want her? He had no idea. His throat was dry. And the black girl stood there, with the chain in the palm of her hand.

He came up to her and stroked her shoulder again. He let his hand slip slowly down to her breasts and circle around them.

She didn't encourage him or discourage him. She looked at the chain.

"Come here."

He drew her toward the mattress on the extended rails of the cot. She followed him.

"Are you . . ."

He wanted to ask her if she was a virgin, because that would have stopped him. She couldn't be made to understand.

"Sit."

And, pressing down on her shoulders, he forced her to sit on the bed. Then, very embarrassed, he went for a sip of whiskey.

At last, with a brutal movement, he slammed the unlatched door of the hut.

II

THERE had been a serious incident and Timar was in a bad mood. They'd been shooting some rapids.

The paddlers, in their excitement, were putting everything they could into it, their mouths wide with silent laughter even as they struggled to catch their breath. They were making tremendous speed. The men were keeping an eye on the eddies at a bend in the river. They intended to clear them in one go.

But the current took them close to a tree branch, its leaves outspread like a small island. The canoe could still avoid it. But instead, in a spirit of fun, the blacks all crowded to one side and paddled furiously.

Their large eyes shone with childish glee, as they looked back and forth between the eddies, the branch, and the white man. They wanted to cut close to the branch: it was going to be a thrill.

Most of the branch was behind them now, but before they passed there was a crash. The canoe rose out of the water.

Timar didn't have time to get up or to realize what was happening. It wasn't all that serious. The boat had struck a submerged part of the branch, but it didn't tip over and the men worked together to right it.

The canoe was nearly half full of water. Timar was sitting in it.

Suddenly he was furious. He swore at the blacks, who couldn't understand. He was all the more furious because he was wet and miserable.

He was out of cigarettes—that was another reason. In the morning, when he'd woken up in the hut, he'd realized that he'd spent the night with a black girl. She had left—he didn't know when.

He'd headed down to the waiting canoe with his men. The villagers were standing by the water with their children. Timar's girl was also there. She was too scared to leave the crowd, to approach him, to make a sign of greeting.

He'd been about to stop for her when he changed his mind. He took his place in the canoe while the blacks climbed in, paddles in hand, one behind the other.

The girl was still standing in the sunlit clearing. She moved away from the crowd and looked at him.

Twelve paddles plunged into the water; at one stroke the canoe was fifty yards out, right in midstream. It seemed to Timar that only then did the girl raise her arm, reaching out ever so slightly, in an incomplete gesture of farewell.

———

The crash had nearly staved in one side of the canoe. Now there was a man bailing it out with both hands.

Timar watched him at it for a long time then took out one of his remaining cans. He dumped its contents into the river and handed it over.

Suddenly all eyes were turned on him in total astonishment. The blacks knew that a can of pâté cost twelve francs—nearly two weeks' work for them. The man scooping away with the can could hardly get enough of dipping it into the sun-dappled water. The others watched with envy.

Timar was no longer thinking about them. He was increasingly preoccupied as they neared the end of the trip. Adèle must have gotten to Libreville the day before, probably toward midafternoon, since the flatboat had had the advantage of the current. Where had she slept? Who had she had dinner with? What had she been doing all morning?

For the first few hours, he thought about the black girl occasionally. After noon, though, his thoughts turned entirely to Adèle —mostly to the memory of their last night together, side by side in bed, in the darkness, looking at the ceiling and pretending to be asleep but listening for each other with their every sense on the alert.

He ate a banana. He didn't know when they'd get there and couldn't ask the man with the bad teeth. The hours passed slowly. Twice they stopped the canoe to make some adjustments to his leaf shelter. Another time he snarled, "What are you waiting for? Sing!"

The blacks didn't understand, so he started to sing the song from the day before. They looked at one another, enormously relieved. The puny fellow started out with a couplet that was even longer and more flowing than anything Timar had heard before.

He didn't pay any attention. After five minutes, he didn't even know they were singing. Why had Bouilloux come to the concession? Why had Adèle left without telling him?

He fell asleep two or three times, but only briefly. He felt a painful drowsiness brought on by the heat and the motion of the canoe. At last the sun sank behind the trees. There was a short dusk, a semblance of coolness, a less brutal glare in which things regained some of their color. Fifteen minutes later it was night and they still hadn't reached Libreville. Timar was furious—all the more so because there was no way for him to ask a question.

They'd been traveling in the dark for an hour when they spotted a red and a green light. Higher up, in the sky, something was shining that wasn't a star. At the same time, they heard a record player and noises on a wooden floor.

The bulk of a cargo ship rose beside the canoe, which had reached the mouth of the river—the place where Timar had seen the other ship being loaded with logs. The record was over, but they'd forgotten to turn the record player off—you could hear the needle skipping.

A blinding light. It swept the water a few times before shining on the canoe and following them. The light came from the captain's gangway. Three men, their elbows on the rail, watched the canoe with the white man in it go by.

"Ahoy!" cried a voice.

Timar didn't reply—he couldn't have said why. He sat glumly in his corner. When the canoe crossed a sandbar and began to pitch, he gave a start.

Before him was the ocean; to the right was a string of lights, a waterfront like every other waterfront in the world, like a real European waterfront, with car lights slipping along into the night.

———

They beached their vessel among the fishing canoes near the place where the market was held every morning. Blacks dressed like whites, others in Arab garb, strolled the esplanade. Timar felt like he was returning from a long voyage.

The electric lights made the red of the dirt road look darker; by contrast the vegetation was the green of glazed china. The whole landscape looked like stage scenery—especially the palms, whose leaves, lit from below, made velvety black silhouettes against the sky.

And there were noises, voices, footsteps, squeals, unfamiliar people walking by, a car with occupants who didn't even wonder about this traveler emerging out of the night.

The three blacks who were naked wrapped their waists in cloth while the others hauled the canoe onto the beach. Timar couldn't make up his mind what to do. Should he tell the blacks to go back to the concession? Or should he keep them here with him? How would he feed them or house them? How would they manage in a city? He went up to the puny fellow with the rotten teeth and made an effort to ask, "Can you sleep here on the beach?"

Timar put a hand to his cheek, bent his head, and closed his eyes.

The black smiled and made a reassuring gesture.

"See madame!" he said.

He'd go see Adèle—she was the one who counted. Timar was just a passenger. In the hierarchy of beings, he was only some sort of protégé of madame's. He wasn't even a real settler, since he didn't speak the local tongue and hadn't shot down the ducks flying over the canoe. He'd given away cigarettes. He hadn't hit anyone. He hadn't pointed out the places to stop at. He was an amateur, a mere passerby.

"Me see madame!"

Timar turned his back to the black and reached the road lit by electric lights. His pants were stained and wrinkled from the accident in the canoe, and he had a three-day growth of beard. A car drove up just as Timar emerged into the glowing circle cast by a streetlight, and he heard the engine slow down. Someone peered at him through the glass; he recognized the chief of police, who went on by but turned to look back twice.

Timar was only three hundred yards away from the hotel. In a dark corner, a black woman draped in blue cloth laughed and rubbed up against a well-dressed native. She was on the plump side, like all the women in the city. Her frizzy hair was arranged in a complicated pile, and she'd lost the respect for the white man that was the rule of the jungle and the bush. As Timar passed she looked at him without saying a word. He was barely ten feet away when she burst out laughing.

These were trifling details, nothing more. But they had an effect on Timar. They added to all the other reasons he had to be in a bad mood.

———

Music was coming from the hotel. They were playing a Hawaiian record that Timar had heard fifty times before. There was the click of billiard balls.

He paused for a moment before going in and scowled so as to assume a threatening air, but no one noticed him at all. A logger and the notary clerk with the enormous gut were playing billiards. Their backs were turned, blocking him from the sight of four other men who were leaning together conspiratorially at a table next to the gramophone. The clock showed eleven. There was no one behind the counter. The notary clerk stepped back, bumping into him. He turned around.

"Well! It's you, young man."

Timar sensed the annoyance.

"Hey, everybody!"

And everybody looked at him, not much surprised but definitely hostile. He was a nuisance, it would appear. There was an exchange of glances. Bouilloux, among the four talking at the table, got up, came over, and cried out with fake delight, "Well, what do you know? This is a surprise!"

Timar's arrival was what he'd foreseen and feared the most.

"So, you came by plane?"

"By canoe."

Bouilloux let out a brief whistle of admiration.

"What are you drinking?"

Timar had shaken his outstretched hand reluctantly. He hadn't been up to ignoring it. The players went back to their game of billiards. Someone changed the record on the phonograph.

"Have you eaten?"

"No . . . yes. I'm not hungry."

"I bet, in any case, you haven't taken your quinine the last couple of days. Just look at your eyes!"

The tone was friendly, but veiled. Among the three people remaining at the table, the one-eyed man surveyed Timar grimly, while Maritain got up abruptly. He gave everyone's hand an angry shake.

"It's late—I'm going to bed."

He seemed to be escaping, afraid of a scene he preferred not to witness. For the first time, Timar was at the center of attention— the situation was almost theatrical. He was the character everyone tiptoes around, and he remembered that he was carrying a gun in his pocket.

"Come on, have a drink!"

Bouilloux dragged him over to the counter. From the other side, he filled two glasses with calvados.

"Cheers! Have a seat."

Timar hauled himself up onto one of the stools, drained his glass, and stared stonily at his companion. They weren't going to pull the wool over his eyes! He knew that the billiard game behind his back was only for show, just like the conversation going on by the phonograph off to the right.

———

Only one thing mattered to anyone: Bouilloux and him; or, rather, their fight.

"Another of the same!" he said, holding out his glass.

And Bouilloux hesitated for a second. He was scared. Timar found himself hamming up his threatening appearance and tough talk. He was acting a lot more confident than he felt.

"Adèle?"

And Bouilloux, with the bottle of calvados in his hand, was also playacting—to gain time.

"Still as much in love as ever? Ha! Ha! You two must be getting along just great up there, with no one to bother you!"

It was wrong, all wrong!

"Where is she?"

"Where is she? You're asking me where she is?"

"She isn't here?"

"Why would she be here? Cheers! So tell me, how long did it take to come downriver by canoe?"

"It doesn't matter. You mean Adèle didn't come to the hotel?"

"I didn't say that. Maybe she did, but she isn't here right now."

Timar had taken the bottle from Bouilloux's hand and poured himself a third glass. Suddenly he wheeled around on the billiards players, catching them by surprise as they were standing there eavesdropping.

"The game's yours! Nice shooting," the notary clerk said too loudly.

Timar had never felt so nervous and yet so clearheaded at the same time. He felt capable of anything, and of pulling it off with complete coolness. He looked at Bouilloux again. He imagined his appearance was terrifying, not realizing that he looked ravaged by fever. What had shocked Bouilloux so much was his pallor, his shot nerves. The logger picked up the two glasses and said, "Come on, young man. Let's talk."

He led him to a corner in the café where they wouldn't be overheard. He set the bottle and glasses on the table, rested his elbows on it, and stretched out a hand toward Timar.

The guests at the other table left, mumbling, "Till tomorrow, Louis. Good night, all."

Their footsteps could be heard outside. Only the billiard players were left—so animated that it looked suspicious.

"Keep calm. This is no time to do something stupid."

The tone was patronizing, but so warm that it reminded Timar of the voices of some priests he'd known when he was a teenager.

"I'm not playing games. We're both grown men."

He looked at his companion's face, sipped his drink, and took back the bottle Timar had commandeered.

"Not now!"

The masks were in their places on the pastel walls. Nothing had changed in the café except for the fact that Adèle, wearing her black silk dress and serious look, was no longer behind the counter, absorbed in her accounts, her chin on her folded hands while she stared off into space.

"The business is going to court tomorrow. Get it?"

His face was very close to Timar's. It was a strange face. Seen up close, it wasn't as brutish as Timar had imagined. Again he was reminded of one of his confessors, who'd had the same gruff voice.

"Everything's set. There's no reason for Adèle to worry. Only it took a lot of doing."

"Where is she?"

"I'm telling you, I don't know. You mustn't come up at the

assizes. It would be better yet if no one even knew you were in Libreville. Don't you get it? Adèle's a good girl—who doesn't deserve eight to ten years of hard labor."

It was hallucinatory: Timar heard the words and understood them, but at the same time he had the impression of seeing through them, as if through bars.

Adèle was a good girl—that's how they talked about her! And they'd slept with her, for God's sake! They were all friends—all part of the same crew, and he was in their way.

Like an angry child who won't listen, he repeated, "Where is she?"

Bouilloux almost gave up. He drained his glass but forgot to prevent Timar from refilling his.

"Listen—the whites here, we stick together. What she did is what she had to do. It doesn't do any good to talk about it. Once again, I'm telling you everything's set—there's nothing you can do but wait and hope things turn out all right."

"When you were her lover, did—"

"No, my boy, no!"

"You told me—"

"It's not the same thing! You have to try to understand, because the situation is serious. I said I'd slept with Adèle. So did a lot of people. That has nothing to do with it."

Timar laughed bitterly.

"Nothing to do with it, I said. And that's why, now, I'm not going to . . ."

He saw how pale Timar was and how he was clenching his fists and hurried on: "There are things in life that sometimes you just have to do. Adèle, back then, had Eugène's full support. The proof it wasn't the same all those times is that Eugène never got jealous. He knew what was necessary."

Timar laughed. He wasn't sure that he wasn't going to break down sobbing with humiliation.

"We here—and the big shots like the governor and company—it was all like a favor she was doing us, the cost of doing business."

Bouilloux's voice turned hard, almost threatening.

"I'd known Adèle for ten years. So! With you, I think, it was the first time. And if I'd known anything about it, I would have done my best to stop it. So there!"

His tone became passionate.

"It was pure chance that Eugène died that night, because if he hadn't I'm certain things would have turned out badly. Don't you see yet? Do I have to dot the i's? I swear: Adèle's in danger. It's a miracle that she's almost in the clear—almost, because it's tomorrow that'll settle the matter one way or the other. So once again I'm telling you that there are some of us here who aren't going to allow..."

He fell silent. Had he thought he'd said too much? Or was he horrified by the sight of Timar, his pale face with its feverish red patches, his shining eyes and blue lips? Those emaciated fingers trembling on the table.

"It doesn't do any good to speak ill of someone. Adèle knows what she's doing."

The billiard balls were still clicking; the two men went on diligently circling the green felt.

"So she's got her plan. Tomorrow night, everything will be over. She can go back up there with you. As to knowing whether she should have left Libreville and all, that's her business."

"Where is she?"

"Where is she? I don't know! And no one here has the right to ask her, get it? Least of all you. Where is she? Probably between someone's sheets, trying to save her skin!"

Bouilloux turned abruptly to the boy standing motionless by the counter.

"Close the place up!"

Then he turned to the players.

"Hey you, get out!"

He was the one who was angry now. Timar didn't know what to say. His hand itched with his desire to pull out his revolver. He heard the sound of the shutters closing, the last guests going off.

Bouilloux stood, almost as worked up as Timar. He leaned over him from above, dominating him with his bulk.

"If she has to do that to save her skin, are you going to get in the way?"

His fists were clenched and he was ready to strike. Timar, for his part, was thinking seriously about shooting.

But no—the brute regained self-control, even warmed up. He put his hand on the young man's shoulder.

"Look, my boy, don't start getting any funny ideas. We're going quietly off to bed. And tomorrow night it'll all be over. You can go back up there, the two of you, and love each other in peace."

Timar poured himself one last glass of liquor and gulped it down. He still looked troubled and anxious, but when Bouilloux pushed him toward the stairs, he didn't resist.

"She's a woman you have to take your hat off to," the logger said from behind him.

Timar never found out who put the candle in his hand or how he made it up to his room or why, when he fell fully dressed on the bed, he tore the mosquito net down.

All he remembered were his great convulsive sobs and waking up with a start when the candle had gone out. He clutched the pillow in his arms as if it had been Adèle.

12

THE COURTHOUSE, like the cemetery, had a provisional flavor, an atmosphere of anything goes, a contempt for tradition. Probably that was why it made Timar think of the burial of Eugène Renaud.

No molding, no dark wood paneling, nothing to give the décor the wonted solemnity. The great bare room might as well have been a factory. The walls were peeling in the heat. There were four openings out onto the veranda, where at least two hundred blacks —blacks dressed city-style along with naked blacks from the bush —were pressed tightly together, some standing, others seated on the ground.

There were no chairs or benches for the spectators inside, and no box for the accused—nothing that makes a court a court. A rope was the only thing separating the officers of the court from the crowd, though almost all of the whites had been admitted into the reserved section.

The blacks, some Spaniards and Portuguese, and a couple of Frenchmen who'd arrived late, like Timar, were on the other side of the rope.

The judge was set to preside over the proceedings from behind a table covered with a green cloth. Were those the assistant magistrates around him? Was he the only judge? The one writing had to be the court clerk. But what were the prosecutor and chief of police doing there, sitting on wicker chairs, their legs sprawled out in front of them? And all those other people Timar didn't know who'd gotten seats?

The windows were open and the blacks on the veranda were

profiled against the light, motionless. All the white men were in linen suits. They wore their sun helmets as a protection from the glare.

People were smoking, getting comfortable.

Lost among the blacks, Timar looked for Adèle a long time before spotting her.

Only in the morning had he managed to fall asleep. Bouilloux, no doubt intentionally, had failed to wake him, and when he'd opened his eyes, it was ten. He'd gone downstairs without shaving and found nobody in the house but the boy. Timar had run to the courthouse, his suit wrinkled and his cheeks covered with stubble. He hadn't had any coffee. He'd pushed his way through the crowd of blacks and into the courthouse, and it had taken him a long time to get the hang of things, to see and understand what was going on.

The whites, without exception, seemed overwhelmed by the heat. In front of the cord, in the very front row, a half-naked black with the fat face of someone from the bush was plaintively droning on with the occasional timid gesture of his rose-colored palm, though standing rigidly at attention throughout.

Was anyone listening? The whites were chatting with one another. From time to time the judge turned toward the windows and shouted something; the black crowd withdrew a little before pressing forward again moments later.

Timar didn't understand what the man was saying. He didn't know who he was. But now, not far from the prosecutor, he spotted Adèle's black dress and the corner of her profile. She hadn't seen him yet. She was signaling to someone else.

The black droned on, rattling off sentences in his pitiful voice. On the wall there was a large white clock of the sort found in government offices. The hands advanced with a jerk. A boy carrying a tray with glasses, a siphon, and a bottle made his way up to the judge. He set the tray down in front of him, and the men around the table all had a drink while ignoring the black man. Adèle had just seen Timar. White as the clock and holding her breath, she looked at him from afar. He fixed her with a malevolent stare.

There was a strong smell from all the blacks crowded together. Timar hadn't had anything to eat or drink. He was starting to feel dizzy, all the more so because he'd been on his feet the whole time and had to stand on tiptoe in order to get a real view.

"Good!" the judge suddenly declared, as the clock marked 10:45. "Silence!"

The black man didn't understand but fell silent instinctively.

"Tell us what he said!"

This was addressed to another black, in white pants and a black vest, wearing a plastic dress collar and glasses—the interpreter. His voice was deep and serious, like far-off thunder.

"He says that he has never laid eyes on Thomas, given that they do not come from the same village, and that he did not even know that Thomas existed."

That sentence alone took three minutes to emerge from the translator's mouth. The judge shouted, "Louder!"

"He says it is because of the goats he demanded from his brother-in-law, after his wife ran off with a man from another village. She was his first wife, one of the chief's daughters, and she told everyone that . . ."

No one was paying any attention. Timar couldn't follow, anymore than the others could, the tenuous thread of a speech whose every other word escaped him. He looked at Adèle. He wondered who she'd spent the night with.

Was she still naked under her dress? Had a man seen her thighs slipping out slowly from under the black silk, her white thighs and supple stomach, her slightly liquid breasts?

"They didn't want to give him back the goats, and . . ."

Suddenly four blacks were all talking at the same time, in dialect, arguing with the accused, arguing among themselves. Their voices were sharp. The accused, wearing a loincloth, looked on in bewilderment.

If you stopped paying close attention for a few moments, the scene lost any semblance of reality; it was a crazy nightmare, a weird parody. On the table covered with the green cloth was a bottle of whiskey. The whites offered one another cigarettes and talked about something else.

Bouilloux was in attendance, along with three other loggers and the notary clerk. They were a distinct group, between the blacks and the officers of the court, standing next to a window and against the cord. Bouilloux was the first to shout, "Enough!"

Other whites took up the cry, "Enough!"

The judge shook a little bell, a cheap toy for a child, not what you'd expect in a court.

"We still need to hear from the woman Amami. Where is the woman Amami?"

Hands pushed her through the crowd of blacks to a place just short of the rope. She was an old black woman. Her breasts sagged. There were tattoos in heavy relief on her chest and stomach, and her head was shaved.

She stood where she'd been left, not saying anything, not seeing anything, and Timar was troubled by a vague impression. He saw the woman in profile, then in partial profile, and it brought back the girl he'd slept with in the village on the river. Weren't the features the same? The outline of the shoulders and hips? Could this woman be the other one's mother?

In which case, the accused, the small man who'd talked for so long without anyone listening—wouldn't he be the father?

Timar compared the couple to his glorious vision of the girl, her body that was both so slender and so full. They were a pitiful sight—more meagerly dressed than anyone. The old woman's skin looked ashen.

They stood a yard apart from each other. Timar saw them look at each other and realized that they had no idea where they were, or what they were doing, or why, most of all, they'd become the object of everyone's hatred. The husband especially, who had a flat upturned nose and beady red eyes, was casting fitful, almost crazed glances around the room.

No one paid attention. At the same moment, Timar became aware of Bouilloux giving him meaningful looks, even motioning with his head, as if to say, half in pleading and half in threat, "Keep your cool!"

Then the woman began to speak—in a monotone, as if each syllable were of equal weight. At the same time, she kept tying and untying her scanty loincloth. And to give herself confidence she trained her eyes on a precise point on the wall, right next to the clock, where there was the stain of a swatted fly.

Out one window Timar recognized the chief paddler; he smiled broadly at him. The heat grew ever more intense. The crowd of bodies, bodies of whites and bodies of blacks, seemed wrapped in an actual cloud, the bland sweat of the whites and the acrid sweat of the blacks mixed with the stench of pipes and cigarettes.

From time to time people made a quiet departure. They returned shortly, after running to the hotel to quench their thirst.

Timar was hot, thirsty, and hungry, but his nerves were so tightly strung that he was able to hold on. He kept trying to catch Adèle's eye, but she looked away. A white man he didn't know was whispering in her ear. She was pale, and there were circles under her eyes.

He was furious and yet full of pity for her; he couldn't sort out his contradictory emotions. For example, the idea that she'd spent the night with someone else made him want to kill her but also to take her tenderly in his arms, weeping over what fate had brought them to.

He heard the voice of the black woman. They were letting her talk on and on, perhaps out of laziness—in order to delay the moment of decision. He saw her shaved old woman's head, her sagging breasts. Her legs were spindly, her knees somewhat turned in.

She spoke without pause, stumbling over her words and swallowing her saliva, fiercely determined to make herself understood and believed. She didn't act like a white woman; she didn't try to engage their sympathy. She never raised her voice. And, instead of crying or fainting, she made it a point of honor to stand as stiff as a statue.

The only human thing about her was her tone of voice, like a bored priest's, those identical syllables that—if you didn't pay attention—became a murmur as indistinct as the sound of rain on a window.

The tension made Timar clench his fists. Her voice pained him, like one of those sad lullabies that country wet nurses still sang. There was something spellbinding about this terrible and nostalgic music, while not a muscle stirred in her face; he was more and more convinced that once again he was seeing that other face, the younger one's, turned toward him as the canoe was leaving the village, and then the motion of her arm, which she'd hardly dared to lift.

Other images crowded in, and he was surprised at how sharp they were. The dozen pairs of eyes fixed on him as the paddles rose and fell; their song—also like a lament—rising into the sultry air. And the hangdog look of the men the moment they struck the branch and Timar lost his temper.

His chest hurt. Was it from hunger or thirst? His knees shook from standing on tiptoe for so long. Suddenly he had an idea. It was his turn to shout, "Enough! Get it over with!"

At that moment, the judge happened to ring his ridiculous little bell. The woman didn't understand; she raised her voice to make herself heard over it. She didn't want to stop speaking. The interpreter spoke up and she raised her voice even louder, never moving, droning on in a tone of despair.

It was like the *Parce Domine* that they would sing three times in a row in church in times of disaster, to different notes, each time more loudly.

Now her voice rang out. She was talking faster. She wanted to tell everything—everything!

"Remove her!"

Other blacks, policemen, who had been carefully dressed by
the whites in dark-blue uniforms topped off with Zouave caps,
dragged the woman away through the crowd. Did she really know
why they'd brought her here or why they were forcing her to leave?
She didn't stop—she went on speechifying to herself.

Timar's glance met Adèle's, and he could tell that she was really
starting to panic. He never guessed that it was because of his own
appearance! His exhaustion and sickness, his struggles, the heat—
everything, absolutely everything could be read in his ravaged,
deathly pale face and feverish eyes—eyes that no longer settled on
anything, but flitted back and forth from white to black, from the
clock to the fly-specked wall.

He was covered in cold sweat. His breath came with difficulty,
and he couldn't fix his thoughts anymore than his glance. But he
had to think; it was urgent; it was absolutely necessary.

"Tell us what she said. Make it short! That was really something! Make it short!"

"She said it isn't true."

The interpreter was sure of himself, flush with self-importance.
Murmurs came from the windows and the judge tinkled his bell,
shouting, "Silence! Or I'll clear the court!"

Other blacks took the witness stand of their own accord; the
judge regained his composure and leaned forward, placing his elbows on the table.

"You, can you speak French?"

"Yes, sir!"

"What makes you think Amami killed Thomas?"

"Yes, sir!"

He pronounced it "suh."

These were the two supporting witnesses. Timar understood
everything. Even better—he could now reconstruct the events as
they had happened one by one. While he was in the village, gazing
at that good-looking naked girl, Adèle had gone to see the chief in
his hut and offered him money in exchange for his producing a
guilty party from among his people. She'd left the gun with him.

It was so simple. The chief had selected the person he liked the least, a black who'd married his daughter and then, when she left him, had the effrontery to demand his bride-price back. The bride-price was some goats and hoes. Five hoes! Five pieces of iron! Two other blacks also testified—men to whom promises had been given. They wanted to earn their pay.

"Yes, sir!"

"But that's not what I'm asking you. When did you come to believe that Amami had murdered Thomas?"

And the judge, exasperated, said, "Interpreter, translate the question."

They went back and forth forever in the native tongue. Finally, they had to be interrupted; the interpreter, unperturbed, translated: "He says Amami has always been considered a bandit."

It was so tense Timar wanted to scream. Amami had stayed after his wife was dragged away. He looked at his accusers in a daze; he tried to speak, but they wouldn't let him. He no longer understood. He was drowning.

Was it really his daughter that Timar had slept with? He blushed at the thought that she was a virgin and that he'd taken her anyway, roughly, with, for an instant, the feeling that he was taking his vengeance on all of Africa.

"So in fact this very gun was found in his hut?"

The judge displayed a pistol. Timar felt Adèle looking at him. So were Bouilloux, the one-eyed man, and the fat notary clerk.

Because he couldn't see himself, he didn't understand. He couldn't see why, in spite of the gravity of the moment, Bouilloux was shoving his way through the crowd of blacks to get to him.

He didn't realize that even the blacks around him were looking at him with apprehension and astonishment. His breath whistled feverishly. He squeezed his hands until his knuckles cracked.

"They both confirm that this is the gun they found. Everyone has sworn to the same. No other white has been to the village since the crime."

The black with the flat, upturned nose directed an anguished, pleading look at the interpreter. He, too, resembled the girl; his skin was also gray and ashen.

The logger and the fat notary clerk watched Bouilloux wade through the crowd toward his goal. On the official side of the rope, the prosecutor and Adèle were talking in low voices and looking at Timar. Suddenly a hand seized Timar's arm; it was Bouilloux.

A voice said, "Careful, now."

Careful of what? Of who? It was driving him mad. For a few seconds, Timar became one with the miserable, half-naked black struggling against the crowd, surrounded by, hunted by, overwhelmed by it.

They were hunting him down, too! They'd sent Bouilloux over to corner him! The logger's steely fingers dug into his arm.

Adèle was looking at him. The prosecutor was looking at him. Even the judge looked up nervously, sensing danger in the air, but all he did was take a sip of whiskey.

Was the black man having the same reaction, feeling the same terror at that moment? The sense that everything was turning against him, that he was being crushed, as if all these bodies, white and black, were circling in to smother him? He continued speaking in the midst of the uproar, talking to himself in a shrill voice, over and over repeating his story that no one wanted to hear.

Timar's nerves were totally shot, and in spite of Bouilloux's bone-crushing grip on his arm, in spite of Adèle and her stare, in spite of the prosecutor, who was smiling at him, Timar shouted, actually shouted, making himself as tall as possible, his face sweaty but drained of blood, his throat so tight that the words hurt him coming out: "It's not true! It's not true! He didn't kill him! It was . . ."

Who cared? It was time for it all to be over! It was time!

He sobbed, "It was her! And you know it!"

With a flip of the wrist, Bouilloux threw him to the ground, where he collapsed amid a throng of black legs and feet.

13

IN A LOW, sneering voice, he said, "It's obvious! It doesn't exist!"

Two passengers turned to look and he looked back unblinkingly. He even gave a shrug—they were government officials, nothing more. The packet boat, having pulled in its launches, was slowly leaving Libreville's outer harbor. Timar was seated at the bar just behind the first-class section. Suddenly he calmed down. He had just realized that he was looking for the last time at the yellow line of the beach, the darker line of vegetation, the red roofs, the jaunty palms.

He was gaunt and his face twitched. He wore a constant scowl. He clenched his fists and muttered under his breath even when there were people around.

"Who brought me to the station?"

He knew he was talking nonsense, because there was no train station in Libreville, and he'd been left to go off alone, without anyone to wave a handkerchief after him from the pier. But he liked the word "station" because it put him in mind of departures, the station in La Rochelle, his mother and sister.

He was very tired. Everyone had told him so. That had been after the big fight. Before that, Timar was never known as a troublemaker, especially not a public one. He was a well-brought-up young man, rather retiring by character.

But when Bouilloux had twisted his arm in the middle of that milling throng, he'd known that they were out to get him, and he'd struck out at random. That was what happened. The teeming mass—blacks and whites all mixed up together—had spilled out onto the road, and Timar's face had been scratched. He was bleeding. He'd lost his sun helmet and was sunburned.

He'd seen fights before, but he'd never been in one. He usually did his best to keep his distance, but this time he'd been right at the center. He'd noticed that the blows hurt a lot less than he would have thought and that it didn't take any courage to fight. Everyone was against him? Then he'd strike back against everyone. He'd hit out and kept hitting until, somehow, he'd found himself in the shady interior of the police station.

He recognized the bands of light and shadow, the table where they drank whiskey. He was sitting in a chair and the police chief was standing, giving him a peculiar look. Timar was so astonished that he ran his hand over his forehead and stammered, "I'm sorry. I don't really know what happened. They were out to get me."

And he smiled a small polite smile. The police chief didn't smile: he looked at him with cold curiosity.

"Thirsty?"

He would have spoken like that to a black or a dog. He gave him some water, nothing else, and went back to pacing the room.

Timar wanted to stand up.

"Stay there!"

"What are we waiting for?"

It was unsettling. A little more and it would be weird.

"Sit down!"

His question hadn't deserved an answer—once again he saw himself as the victim of a plot.

"Come in, doctor. I hope you're doing well. You've heard what happened?"

The police chief indicated Timar with his eyes. The doctor spoke softly.

"What are we going to do?"

"He should be arrested. After committing an outrage like that..."

The doctor snorted. He addressed Timar coldly, just like the chief of police. "So you were the one who caused all the trouble?"

At the same time, he was lifting of Timar's eyelid and lowering it, taking his pulse for a few seconds, and examining him from head to foot.

"Uh-huh," he growled out.

Then he turned to the police chief. "May I have a brief word with you?"

Out on the veranda, they whispered together. When the chief returned, he scratched his head and shouted to a boy, "Get the governor on the telephone!"

He spoke into the receiver. "Hello! Just as we thought, yes. Shall I bring him? Even if it weren't for this there'd be nothing else to do; the loggers would never stand for it. You'll meet us there?"

He picked up his sun helmet and said to Timar, "Coming?"

And Timar followed, surprised to find himself so docile. He was numb. He'd never imagined such torpor, an emptiness filling his limbs and head. He followed the chief of police into the hospital courtyard without asking why they were taking him there. The governor's car was already parked outside. In a very clean room, much cleaner than the rooms at the hotel, they found the governor. He didn't shake the hand Timar extended.

"I don't know, young man, if you quite realize the significance of what you've done."

No! Honestly speaking, he didn't and he never would. He'd fought back. He remembered a black man and a black woman who were chanting something in a smotheringly hot room; Adèle looking at him from afar, trying to tell him something.

"Do you have any money?"

"I think there's still some in the bank."

"In that case, I'm going to give you a bit of advice. There's a boat leaving for France in two days, the *Foucault*. Get on that boat and get out of here."

Timar started to put up a struggle. He spoke slowly, trying to maintain his dignity. "I want to talk about this business with Adèle."

"Some other time! Now get in bed!"

They left, the governor and the police chief both equally cold and contemptuous. Timar had slept. He was running a high fever and his head was splitting. He said to the nurse, "It's that nasty little bone, right at the base of the skull."

Now he was on board the ship. There hadn't been a transition. The police chief had visited him in the hospital twice. Timar wanted to know if he could see Adèle.

"Better not."

"What's she saying?"

"Nothing."

"And the doctor? He says I'm crazy, doesn't he?"

That annoyed him. He might look crazy, but he wasn't. He made crazy faces and he acted crazy, and sometimes the thoughts spinning in his head even seemed crazy.

"It doesn't exist!"

No! He was sure of it. The proof was he was completely self-possessed. He'd packed his bags all by himself. He'd noticed that his white suits were missing and had asked for them: he knew that on board everyone wore white until Tenerife.

On the pier at 7 AM, alone with the porters, he gave a snort as he turned to the red dirt road, its border of palm trees standing out against the sky. He'd said, "It doesn't exist!"

It did exist, obviously, though he knew what he meant. But he knew just as well that this was only a passing condition. That was why he wasn't ashamed.

He took his place in the launch. Suddenly, he buried his face in his hands. "Adèle!"

He ground his teeth. Between his fingers, he could see the blacks smiling. The sea was flat.

Now it was over. Africa was out of sight.

The barman came up.

"What can I get you?"

"An orange soda."

From their brief exchange of glances Timar could tell that the barman thought he was crazy, too. They must have forewarned the authorities on board.

"It doesn't exist!"

A train ... what train? Ah, yes—the train from La Rochelle; his sister, waving a handkerchief.

He brooded, seated in a wicker chair. He was dressed in black because they hadn't found his white colonial suit. Still, it made him feel good to be different from the other passengers. There were a lot of military officers—too many of them.

"Too many stripes," he muttered.

And too many government officials! Too many children running around on deck!

What did that make him think of? Ah, yes—Adèle. She always wore black, too. Only she didn't have a child and she was naked under her dress. While the black girl had been naked and without a dress!

He remembered it all very well. Everything! It had been a lot worse than anyone would have ever believed. They wanted to blame the girl's father. Timar had saved him, but they'd banded together to attack him.

Because it was a conspiracy. Everyone was in on it. The governor and the prosecutor and the loggers. And all of them, of course, had slept with Adèle.

People dressed in white paced the deck to kill time.

"Killing? That doesn't exist!"

And suddenly Timar stopped thinking—at least he stopped thinking so fast. His thoughts hung in suspense. He saw himself, dressed in black, his sun helmet dangling from his neck, seated at the bar of a packet boat. He was returning to France.

He must have taken some blows to the head. It was enough to drive him crazy. They thought he was. But it wouldn't last long, he knew. He felt so good that he was just putting off the moment when he'd get better and be entirely back to normal!

It was a little trick he'd taught himself. He thought as hard as he could. He'd close his eyes halfway, letting the images mingle together until they grew distorted as in a dream.

Night fell. Some people at the next table, government officials by the look of them, were playing cards and drinking Pernod. Like in Libreville, at Adèle's! He'd learned how to play those games—it wasn't hard.

Already another night...Yes, it was a couple of weeks later... Just before arriving at the concession...In the flatboat...Yes, an attack of some sort...He'd been in a fight...He'd hit people... They'd put him to bed...

Adèle was lying next to him, naked. They were watching each other. They were both pretending to be asleep, but Timar really did fall asleep. She took advantage of him and ran off. When he woke up—no more Adèle!

The little black girl had been a virgin.

"It doesn't exist!"

People kept walking by, among them a young lieutenant with his sun helmet still on even though the sun had gone down. A captain at the card table said, "Afraid of moonstroke?"

Timar spun around. That was something he'd heard before somewhere, when he was sleeping or out of his mind. They'd said it with the same irony then, which is why he stared hard at the captain, as if he intended to demand an explanation or an apology.

The cardplayers consulted together for a moment in low voices. Then they rose.

"Shall we dress for dinner?"

And Timar, standing on the deck, followed them with a look of contempt.

Alone at his table for dinner, he felt calm and collected. He laughed sarcastically from time to time, since people were glancing at him with a mixture of pity and curiosity. It was on purpose that he kept muttering broken sentences under his breath.

There was a little girl who thought he was funny. Timar liked seeing her hiding behind her napkin and giggling.

It didn't matter. Timar knew that very well. It was like the tides. At a given time, the sea recedes, even if it appears to be in a fury. The whole thing was mathematical.

And in the same way the images were becoming more and more distinct, less jumbled together. Except at night. On two occasions he found himself in tears, sitting up in his bunk and soaked in sweat, his limbs trembling as he felt around for Adèle.

But now things had changed. It was night, and Adèle wasn't there. Or rather she was there but he couldn't touch her, hold her, feel her white breasts.

The black girl was in the bed, too, inert, resigned. That had to be looked into, a decision had to be made. Perhaps go away with Adèle, far off . . .

Oh God, let it all come to an end! No more Africa! No more Gabon! No more okume logs! Let the blacks have the logs and Constantinesco can go look after himself!

Only Adèle mattered, zebra-striped with light and shadow, between clammy sheets. Then he'd listen carefully: she was downstairs; he heard the boy coming and going as he swept up while she did her accounts at the bar.

It was the ship's doctor who woke him, a stupid young man who felt obliged to go on playacting.

"They tell me we're from the same part of the country, so—"

"Where are you from?"

"La Pallice."

"That's not the same part of the country!"

A mile and a half off—but a mile and a half is a mile and a half. Not to mention that he looked like an idiot with his huge, bulging eyes. He wanted to know how Timar was feeling. Oh fine—calm and collected.

"Did you sleep well?"

"No—terribly."

"Clearly you need some medication."

If only they'd leave him in peace! That was all he asked. He didn't need anyone. He certainly didn't need medication. He was smarter than all the doctors in the world!

A lot smarter, too, than even he had been *before*. Because, now —he had antennas. He was aware of things that were too subtle for most people. He was aware of everything, even the future, even the visit the family doctor was sure to pay in La Rochelle, in the little house on the rue Chef-de-Ville—the family doctor who would also say, with a smile on his face, "So, young man, how are we doing today?"

And his mother and his sister and everyone—all worrying over him. And the doctor in the corridor, whispering as he left, "He needs to rest. It won't last."

God! And they'd spoil him. They'd be sure to mention his cousin Blanche, from Cognac, who would materialize one Sunday in a new red dress!

Fine! He'd marry her, damn it. Just to have some peace. He'd take the job at the oil refinery they'd told him about, which actually was in La Pallice. In that neighborhood near the sea, where they'd built those hideous houses for workers. His house would be bigger, with a garden, villa-style. And a motorbike. He'd settle down there and be nice as can be. He'd never wanted anything as much as that. Perhaps he'd even agree to have some children.

The people he ran into on deck or in the music room could tell he had antennas. They turned away with a look of shock. They spoke in an undertone.

"And after?"

The best thing, really the best thing of all, had been when the twelve paddles leaped out of the water at once, and for a split second the twelve black paddlers held their breaths, their eyes fixed on the white man, before all going "Hah" in a deep voice.

And the twelve paddles plunged back into the water. Abdominal muscles strained and rippled, and there were fresh pearls of sweat on their skin and pearls of water splashing around the canoe!

No use talking about it. No one would understand.

Certainly not in his office in La Pallice. Certainly not Blanche, who was a pretty girl.

"It doesn't exist!"

He met the amused eyes of the barman, who said, "How's it going, Mr. Timar?"

"Okay."

"You're going ashore at Cotonou?"

"Ashore? That doesn't exist!"

The barman gave him a complicit smile.

"Can I get you an orange soda?"

"Yes, an orange soda. Indeed! Didn't they forbid me whiskey? Whiskey doesn't exist!"

He said it without conviction, however. There were times like that—he was completely calm and collected, entirely self-possessed, and he saw things in the cold light of day.

But he couldn't! Not yet! Or then ... Maybe, for example, he was capable of suddenly jumping overboard! And yet he knew that he never would.

The ship's bow gracefully split the gray-blue sea. You could sit in the shade in the terrace of the bar. A sailor was painting the inside of the air shafts red.

Timar promised to be good. With Blanche and everyone in La Rochelle and La Pallice. He'd see the ships leaving for Africa. And the young people. And the government officials.

But he wouldn't say a thing, nothing at all. Only sometimes at night, and only at night, he'd suffer from moonstroke—his attack, as they'd say—and that would help him, in the emptiness of his bed, to find once again the too-white flesh of Adèle, and the stifling atmosphere, and the aftertaste of sweat, and the smell of the black paddlers, while his wife in her nightgown brewed him a cup of herbal tea.

People continued to turn their backs on him. But he was so

calm and so good at putting one and one together without any problem or even a trace of worry that he felt obliged to toy with them a bit, if only for show: he would look them in the face with his small, feverish, ironic eyes and he would say out loud, "Africa doesn't exist."

He took care to pace the deck for another quarter of an hour, always repeating, "Africa—it doesn't exist. Africa . . ."

TITLES IN SERIES

J.R. ACKERLEY Hindoo Holiday

J.R. ACKERLEY My Dog Tulip

J.R. ACKERLEY My Father and Myself

J.R. ACKERLEY We Think the World of You

CÉLESTE ALBARET Monsieur Proust

DANTE ALIGHIERI The Inferno

DANTE ALIGHIERI The New Life

WILLIAM ATTAWAY Blood on the Forge

W.H. AUDEN (EDITOR) The Living Thoughts of Kierkegaard

W.H. AUDEN W. H. Auden's Book of Light Verse

DOROTHY BAKER Cassandra at the Wedding

J.A. BAKER The Peregrine

HONORÉ DE BALZAC The Unknown Masterpiece *and* Gambara

MAX BEERBOHM Seven Men

ALEXANDER BERKMAN Prison Memoirs of an Anarchist

ADOLFO BIOY CASARES The Invention of Morel

CAROLINE BLACKWOOD Corrigan

CAROLINE BLACKWOOD Great Granny Webster

MALCOLM BRALY On the Yard

JOHN HORNE BURNS The Gallery

ROBERT BURTON The Anatomy of Melancholy

CAMARA LAYE The Radiance of the King

GIROLAMO CARDANO The Book of My Life

J.L. CARR A Month in the Country

JOYCE CARY Herself Surprised (First Trilogy, Vol. 1)

JOYCE CARY To Be a Pilgrim (First Trilogy, Vol. 2)

JOYCE CARY The Horse's Mouth (First Trilogy, Vol. 3)

BLAISE CENDRARS Moravagine

NIRAD C. CHAUDHURI The Autobiography of an Unknown Indian

ANTON CHEKHOV Peasants and Other Stories

RICHARD COBB Paris and Elsewhere

COLETTE The Pure and the Impure

JOHN COLLIER Fancies and Goodnights

IVY COMPTON-BURNETT A House and Its Head

IVY COMPTON-BURNETT Manservant and Maidservant

BARBARA COMYNS The Vet's Daughter

EVAN S. CONNELL The Diary of a Rapist

JULIO CORTÁZAR The Winners

HAROLD CRUSE The Crisis of the Negro Intellectual

ASTOLPHE DE CUSTINE Letters from Russia

LORENZO DA PONTE Memoirs

ELIZABETH DAVID A Book of Mediterranean Food

ELIZABETH DAVID Summer Cooking

MARIA DERMOÛT The Ten Thousand Things

ARTHUR CONAN DOYLE Exploits and Adventures of Brigadier Gerard

CHARLES DUFF A Handbook on Hanging

J.G. FARRELL Troubles

J.G. FARRELL The Siege of Krishnapur

J.G. FARRELL The Singapore Grip

M.I. FINLEY The World of Odysseus

EDWIN FRANK (EDITOR) Unknown Masterpieces

MAVIS GALLANT Paris Stories

MAVIS GALLANT Varieties of Exile

JEAN GENET Prisoner of Love

P.V. GLOB The Bog People: Iron-Age Man Preserved

EDWARD GOREY (EDITOR) The Haunted Looking Glass

PETER HANDKE A Sorrow Beyond Dreams

ELIZABETH HARDWICK Seduction and Betrayal

ELIZABETH HARDWICK Sleepless Nights

L.P. HARTLEY Eustace and Hilda: A Trilogy

L.P. HARTLEY The Go-Between

NATHANIEL HAWTHORNE Twenty Days with Julian & Little Bunny by Papa

JANET HOBHOUSE The Furies

HUGO VON HOFMANNSTHAL The Lord Chandos Letter

JAMES HOGG The Private Memoirs and Confessions of a Justified Sinner

RICHARD HOLMES Shelley: The Pursuit

WILLIAM DEAN HOWELLS Indian Summer

RICHARD HUGHES A High Wind in Jamaica

RICHARD HUGHES The Fox in the Attic (The Human Predicament, Vol. 1)

RICHARD HUGHES The Wooden Shepherdess (The Human Predicament, Vol. 2)

HENRY JAMES The Ivory Tower

HENRY JAMES The Other House

HENRY JAMES The Outcry

RANDALL JARRELL (EDITOR) Randall Jarrell's Book of Stories

DAVID JONES In Parenthesis

ERNST JÜNGER The Glass Bees

HELEN KELLER The World I Live In

MURRAY KEMPTON Part of Our Time: Some Ruins and Monuments of the Thirties

DAVID KIDD Peking Story

TÉTÉ-MICHEL KPOMASSIE An African in Greenland

D.B. WYNDHAM LEWIS AND CHARLES LEE (EDITORS) The Stuffed Owl:
An Anthology of Bad Verse

GEORG CHRISTOPH LICHTENBERG The Waste Books

H.P. LOVECRAFT AND OTHERS The Colour Out of Space

ROSE MACAULAY The Towers of Trebizond

JANET MALCOLM In the Freud Archives

OSIP MANDELSTAM The Selected Poems of Osip Mandelstam

JAMES MCCOURT Mawrdew Czgowchwz

HENRI MICHAUX Miserable Miracle

JESSICA MITFORD Hons and Rebels

NANCY MITFORD Madame de Pompadour

ALBERTO MORAVIA Boredom

ALBERTO MORAVIA Contempt

ÁLVARO MUTIS The Adventures and Misadventures of Maqroll

L.H. MYERS The Root and the Flower
DARCY O'BRIEN A Way of Life, Like Any Other
YURI OLESHA Envy
IONA AND PETER OPIE The Lore and Language of Schoolchildren
BORIS PASTERNAK, MARINA TSVETAYEVA, AND RAINER MARIA RILKE
Letters: Summer 1926
CESARE PAVESE The Moon and the Bonfires
CESARE PAVESE The Selected Works of Cesare Pavese
LUIGI PIRANDELLO The Late Mattia Pascal
ANDREI PLATONOV The Fierce and Beautiful World
J.F. POWERS Morte d'Urban
J.F. POWERS The Stories of J. F. Powers
J.F. POWERS Wheat That Springeth Green
RAYMOND QUENEAU We Always Treat Women Too Well
RAYMOND QUENEAU Witch Grass
RAYMOND RADIGUET Count d'Orgel's Ball
JEAN RENOIR Renoir, My Father
FR. ROLFE Hadrian the Seventh
WILLIAM ROUGHEAD Classic Crimes
CONSTANCE ROURKE American Humor: A Study of the National Character
GERSHOM SCHOLEM Walter Benjamin: The Story of a Friendship
DANIEL PAUL SCHREBER Memoirs of My Nervous Illness
JAMES SCHUYLER Alfred and Guinevere
LEONARDO SCIASCIA The Day of the Owl
LEONARDO SCIASCIA Equal Danger
LEONARDO SCIASCIA The Moro Affair
LEONARDO SCIASCIA To Each His Own
LEONARDO SCIASCIA The Wine-Dark Sea
VICTOR SEGALEN René Leys
VICTOR SERGE The Case of Comrade Tulayev
SHCHEDRIN The Golovlyov Family
GEORGES SIMENON Dirty Snow
GEORGES SIMENON The Man Who Watched Trains Go By
GEORGES SIMENON Monsieur Monde Vanishes
GEORGES SIMENON Three Bedrooms in Manhattan
GEORGES SIMENON Tropic Moon
MAY SINCLAIR Mary Olivier: A Life
TESS SLESINGER The Unpossessed: A Novel of the Thirties
CHRISTINA STEAD Letty Fox: Her Luck
STENDHAL The Life of Henry Brulard
ITALO SVEVO As a Man Grows Older
HARVEY SWADOS Nights in the Gardens of Brooklyn
A.J.A. SYMONS The Quest for Corvo
EDWARD JOHN TRELAWNY Records of Shelley, Byron, and the Author
LIONEL TRILLING The Middle of the Journey
IVAN TURGENEV Virgin Soil
JULES VALLÈS The Child

EDWARD LEWIS WALLANT The Tenants of Moonbloom

ROBERT WALSER Jakob von Gunten

ROBERT WALSER Selected Stories

SYLVIA TOWNSEND WARNER Lolly Willowes

SYLVIA TOWNSEND WARNER Mr. Fortune's Maggot *and* The Salutation

ALEKSANDER WAT My Century

C.V. WEDGWOOD The Thirty Years War

SIMONE WEIL AND RACHEL BESPALOFF War and the Iliad

GLENWAY WESCOTT Apartment in Athens

GLENWAY WESCOTT The Pilgrim Hawk

REBECCA WEST The Fountain Overflows

PATRICK WHITE Riders in the Chariot

ANGUS WILSON Anglo-Saxon Attitudes

EDMUND WILSON Memoirs of Hecate County

EDMUND WILSON To the Finland Station

GEOFFREY WOLFF Black Sun